The Same Cloth

The Same Cloth

Geraldine McMenamin

ROBERT HALE · LONDON

ISBN 978-0-7090-8673-4

Robert Hale Limited
Clerkenwell House
Clerkenwell Green
London EC1R 0HT

www.halebooks.com

2 4 6 8 10 9 7 5 3 1

To my Dad, John McMenamin,
who would appreciate the title

Typeset in 11/13½pt Plantin.
Printed and bound in Great Britain by
Biddles Limited, King's Lynn

1

The Return

THE SUMMER-HOUSE IS a strange name for one of the most unusual buildings I know. It is located in the wooded part of the estate, on a cliff that overhangs a small river.

She had it built in the seventies at a time when she was at her most admired ... a society dame with enough money to spend on an expensive post-modern architect. Few people in the country would have even used architects in those days. But not her, she had to have the very best of everything.

Michael Wright had indeed achieved a classic when he chose steel and glass for what became the most important room on the estate. Enormous steel girders had to be transported, in sections, through the forest, and then welded together before they were secured into the river-bed. These lengthy girders, when welded together, rose sixty feet up the cliff edge and formed the foundations of the structure. Each of the four walls in the rectangular-shaped building was made of flawlessly clear glass that extended from floor to ceiling. The structure started at the end of the forest path and extended through the trees and over the river. It had cost a small fortune to build. 'A scandalous waste', I had heard one of the gardeners say.

To some, when it was first built, it must have seemed odd to use such harsh materials within the gentler surroundings of the wild oak forest and the river-bed. It was a stark contrast, a bold statement of how she could dominate everything and all around her.

Somehow I imagined that would have pleased her. That's how she would have liked to have been perceived ... a hard bitch in a soft world.

Things don't always work out as planned though and with time the summer-house had blended in too well with its surroundings. The trees had grown taller and obscured the view from the inside so that in many ways it felt like an enclosed tree house. Shrubs on the river-bank had wound their way wildly up the cliff edge and were now encroaching on the house corners. Moss had lodged itself successfully on the flat roof. Flowering clematis and vigorous Virginia creeper had engaged with the steel girders as if they were trying to drag the structure back into the forest floor.

No attempt was made to stop this onslaught and I always felt that nature would win out in the end. I imagined some future archaeologist, or an alien being, discovering the summer-house and concluding that the forest had come alive to gobble up the invader.

It was without doubt my favourite place. When I had come back to the estate that summer it was practically abandoned. Its style of architecture had gone out of vogue and it had been built before the concept of insulation had been perfected. It was cold.

She had built a replica Victorian conservatory attached to the main house and that's where she now held her evening soirées. 'The path to the summer-house is so charming but it absolutely ruins ones heels,' I had overheard her say to one of her many visitors.

That suited me just fine. I had practically lived in it for those long summer months when I was forced to come and stay with her. After a long tramp around the estate in the mornings I would spend the day in there painting and listening to U2 and The Virgin Prunes.

I met some local lads from the village and sometimes a gang of them would come along with their girlfriends and sisters and friends and we would all hang out there. I showed them a way to break into the estate so that they didn't have to go past the main house.

In the evenings, if she wasn't around, I would have soirées of my own with stolen beer and home-grown weed. No one ever knew what went on there, or at least if they did I wasn't made aware of it. I was left alone in the summer-house, using it as my refuge, my only solace, my sanity.

It feels strange to be back on the estate again now and even stranger to find that she is not in the main house. She is not languishing about in the grand drawing-room ordering her assistants about, or being rude and intimidating on the phone to one of her many suppliers or staff.

When I call at the main house, Charlie tells me that she has all but moved in there, into the summer-house. She has shunned the luxuries of her own bedroom suite and has insisted on being transported down to the summer-house in a wheelchair. Her bed has been moved along with her toiletries, as well as all the medication and any clothes that she needs.

'It's too cold, Charlie; that can't be good for her that cold summer-house.'

'Oh no, it's all been renovated now,' he tells me. 'She's even made a balcony that goes all around the valley side so that she can sit out and take some air.' I inhale sharply at the thought of what she has done to *my* summer-house.

Charlie gives me all this news in his soft Kerry voice over a cup of tea in the kitchen. I have never understood why he has stayed with her for so long. He is handsome, in his own way, and reliable and capable of any task she ever gives him. He could have worked for anyone. He could have had a family of his own. He could have gone away to America like his brothers. But no, some part of him has remained loyal to her above everything else, and he is still here making arrangements for her till the very end.

He is a shy man and it took me by surprise when I received his call two days ago.

'She doesn't know I am calling you, you understand, don't you, Miss? It's just that ... well ... I know her, I know her right well and I know she'd like to see you.'

Instinctively I knew that I had to make this journey to see her one more time. I hastily made arrangements with my husband to mind our son and leave my hectic life in Dublin to come here, to the kitchen, to have my cup of tea with Charlie and try to be sad.

In a way I am angry that she has any power over me at all. I have to keep reminding myself that she hasn't asked me to come. Would she do the same for me? I ask myself again and again. I don't think so.

Charlie said she would be waking up soon from her afternoon nap and it would be a good time to see her. Now I find myself reluctantly walking back down the forest path. It is such a long time since I have been here that I can barely find my way. I am watching out for the original garish structure at the end of the track and when I don't see it immediately I think I have taken a wrong turn. I retrace my steps and start again and this time I know I am right. Just as I reach the end of the path I catch a glimpse of some reflected light. My God, it's one of the windows, I think to myself. The summer-house is now almost completely obscured by growth. What started years ago has continued unchecked. I am confused. What did Charlie mean when he said it had been renovated?

At least the sliding entrance door is in the same place, but now it moves silently when I open it. It is no longer cold inside. She must have installed heating.

The light is temporarily fading outside as a cloud passes over-head and it takes a moment or two for my eyes to adjust to the inner darkness. I can see her big old iron bed facing the valley window. I walk towards it quietly, afraid to disturb her sleep. I stop a few feet away from the bed, suddenly fearful again as I always was with her. I notice the sound of her breath, and its slow uneasy rattling becomes the loudest sound on earth. I am about to turn tail and run when slowly she opens her eyes and smiles at me. I stand in shock and cannot recognize this new look.

'Darling, am I dreaming or are you really here?' she asks in a low voice.

'No, you're not dreaming; it's me, Mother, it's me.'

2

The Fall

MY VISIT IS BRIEF and I am troubled. I make my way back to the main house in the fading evening light. Charlie meets me as I approach and walks around the back with me and we head towards the kitchen door.

'I stay at the mews house now in what used to be the old stable yard; you remember that, don't you, *a stór*?' He turns his head towards a neatly renovated stone building.

'Yes, yes, of … of course I remember it.' But in truth my memory is very hazy, clouded over like the misty forest that surrounds this big house.

He senses my unease. 'It's all done up now; it's a lovely job. You can have a good look round in the morning and I'm sure you'll remember it better.'

Yes, in the morning everything will seem clearer, I tell myself.

Once in the kitchen Charlie insists that I have some 'tea' and produces a ham salad that Mrs Molloy, the housekeeper, made for me earlier and left in the fridge. He takes out the plate and unwraps the cling film from it. I recognize the willow patterned set from long ago. On the plate there is garden lettuce, baked ham, halved beef tomatoes, white pickled onions and sliced hard-boiled eggs. Every item has been placed separately and, I imagine, carefully on the plate by hands that must now be old and gnarled. I haven't had a salad like this for years. Before he serves it to me, he cuts some brown bread from the fresh loaf on the wire rack, uncovers the butter from the earthenware dish and finally comes to sit with me. The ceremony of it enthrals me and has me wondering of times gone past. At first we eat in silence.

I look around at what is the only familiar room in the main house. The kitchen remains unchanged with the big old pine table and chairs. The good china is on the dresser and there are copper pans hanging down from above the Aga. The cooker is not lit though and somehow the soul of the room is missing.

He begins to chit chat about the house and the staff and the estate. Details that are not important, not now. I am detached. This is his world; she is its centre. I am apart.

Charlie pours me out a cup of tea from a big brown earthenware pot and plonks a large glass of Irish whiskey beside it. At first I decline but, as I know he will, he insists and eventually I accept. I know he wants to talk.

'Did your mother make any sense at all?'

'No, Charlie, I don't know what she was talking about. She was rambling on about all sorts of things I didn't understand. I honestly couldn't work out what she was saying.'

He is disappointed. That much is obvious. I don't know what he was hoping for. Did he think that the past between my mother and I could be reconciled in one brief visit? Nevertheless I sense that he needs to talk about her and I engage him in more conversation.

'Tell me about my mother when she was younger, Charlie. You knew her before we ever moved to Cillindara, didn't you?'

'Ah that was a long time ago now, Miss Helen, another era.'

'Yes but you knew her as a child, didn't you? Long before I came along. Tell me, Charlie. Tell me about Katherine Royston.'

He takes a slug of his whiskey and feigns reluctance at opening up, but I push him gently into a conversation that I know he needs to have.

'We went to the same national school in Kerry, you know in the town of Donntra.'

'No, I didn't know that, Charlie.'

He tells me stories of cycling to school with her and my father

Dan Fitzgerald, my real father as I used to refer to him as a child. I laugh at Charlie's anecdotes speckled with flat tyres and puddles, haystacks and harvest dances. He makes her sound innocent and joyful. Just like any other young girl growing up in post-war rural Ireland. Why does it not fit in with the mother that I know? Why was she so secretive about her youth? I am coming back to visit her at the end of her life and yet I know nothing about the beginning.

'Tell me more, Charlie, please. What did she do when she left school? I feel like I don't even know my own mother.'

Charlie is getting slightly uncomfortable now. Perhaps I should not have been so frank. I pour him another glass of whiskey. He looks resigned.

'Well, your mother was fierce clever, you know, full of brains, and she was determined, too. Sure, look how far she has come. She wasn't going live out her life in a little town at the back end of Mount Brandon, that was for sure.'

'Is that right? Go on, fill me in, Charlie. What did she do after school?'

He takes a sip of whiskey, savours it and looks into the glass for a moment. Then he speaks:

'In those days there was a lot of us that left school early. But not your mother, she went into the nuns in Bandon. That made her a bit different from the rest of us. She finished secondary school and then did a commercial course in Cork city.'

'You mean typing and shorthand?'

'Yes, to be a secretary; that was a good job for girls in those days.'

'And where did she work?'

He looks at me in quizzically, as if I should know all this.

'I don't know, Charlie, honestly I don't.'

'She got a job in Cork city. She worked for legal people, solicitors they were, a family that lived in Montenottee. She loved it up there. It was a father and two sons who ran the practice and they took to your mother straight away. Very respectable family they were, too. She was at all their parties and gatherings. They sort of adopted her as their own. Oh, the stories she used to tell when she came home would dazzle us all. It gave her a taste of what it was like to be rich. That was the start of it.'

'The start of what, Charlie?'

I can see his eyes are welling up. Maybe it is too much for him to be in the past with her now. Still, I press on, curious to fill in the years of my mother's life that I never knew.

'How did she end up going home and marrying a local man? How did we ever get to move to Cillindara?'

But he won't be persuaded. He has composed himself now and will not go any further.

'Another time, Helen, God willing, there's plenty of time. You should spend a few days here and it will all come to light. She wants to see you. She needs to talk to you now, to make up – to make up for whatever has gone before. I know the two of you aren't close, but she is your mother and now is the time to put the past to rest.'

It is obvious then, and why would it not be? The rift between me and her. I have forgotten how odd the relationship between me and my mother must appear to an outsider. The last time I came back to the estate was easily over ten years ago. Could I have been more forgiving of her? Should I have tried harder? Why does she have the power to still make me feel at fault?

He bids me goodnight and tells me to make myself at home in the house. Home is a not a word that I associate with Cillindara. When he leaves I realize that this is the first time I have ever been here alone so I take him at his word and decide to have a good look around.

I climb the stairs from the basement and wander from room to room, whiskey in hand. With each sip it begins to taste warmer, better, like I need some more. I find a cut-glass decanter half full on the sideboard in the formal dining-room and help myself.

I find it curious that for so many years I have carried a picture of this house around in my head but that picture had no clear focus; the camera was at the wrong setting. Whereas everything here used to be posh and expensive and unattainable I now only see its charm and taste and beauty. The William Morris wallpaper, the velvet drapes, the handmade Donegal carpet, the Irish silver, the Derek Hill print. The art collection is sizeable. A Jack Yeats hangs over the fireplace in the hall; is that a le Brocquy in the dining-room? Everything is perfectly placed, put in position a long time ago, and yet I never particularly noticed these things before.

On I wander, across the wide hall with the evening sun squinting through the fanlight up over the wide Georgian door. Through, to the drawing-room with the Parker Knoll couches and the *Country Life* magazines neatly stacked on the coffee table. I feel as if I am in a museum, viewing her life through the series of silver-framed photographs on the mantelpiece. Curious then that she has none of her childhood, as if she only came to life when she married Edgar, my stepfather. I pick up the frames individually and examine each one closely. There are plenty of Edgar and her, mostly in formal clothes, at dinner parties or charity balls. In some of them they are alone, in others surrounded by friends and acquaintances. In all of them he looks important, self-assured, relaxed. I had forgotten how handsome he was. When she first married him I had always imagined him as old, past it, grandfather-like. When I see the photographs of him now I can see that before I had looked at him only through childish eyes. I sigh at the thought of how difficult I made it for him when he married her. I had swayed between being confrontational and sullen. How hard it must have been for him and yet throughout all that time he was forever patient with me. Then I see an older photograph, taken before he married her. It's of him and his only son Julian, the one who died on the Tipperary Hunt. He was such a gorgeous-looking young man. How did Edgar ever carry on without him? I think how different my life would have been if he had lived, if I had ever met him. A shiver runs through me at the thought of ever losing my son Jack and I replace the photograph exactly where it was trying to obliterate the image of the smiling happy Julian from my mind.

I concentrate on images of my mother. She was a strikingly beautiful woman, of that there is no question. Long black hair, almond-shaped green eyes, full lips, and translucent pearly-white skin. In some of the photographs she looks adoringly at Edgar; in one she holds onto his arm; in another she actually holds his hand and there is an innocence in her expression that I have never seen before. She must have been in love with him. That much I can deduce from the images in front of me. But why is the woman in the photographs not the same as the mother I knew? Why is my truth so different from the reality that is presented in front of me? Did she give him all her softness and have none left for me? Is that what happened between us?

As I come to the end of the mantelpiece I realize that there are no photographs of me or my Jack. I would expect that. Even so, it still hurts that she chose to ignore me all these years, that there was no space in her heart for her only child and grandson.

I leave the drawing-room and, wandering on, I find myself in her study, fingering the leather-topped desk, eyeing the wall-to-wall books on the shelves. It is the end of May and night-time has finally drawn in so that I need to turn on a light to continue my casual inspection.

The addition of electric light makes me feel like an intruder now, guilty that I have invaded her private space, nervous that Charlie will think that I am snooping. I am.

The framed painting above the fireplace confuses me when I see it. I am sure it was not there when I was here before. At first I cannot understand why it is familiar, certainly not by a famous artist. It's a vibrant oil with strong colours of a woodland, almost abstract. The trees are native Irish oak. The forest is covered with saplings and large ferns. There is frenzy in it.

Then the startling truth hits: it's mine. Yes, for sure, it's one of the paintings I did that summer messing about around the estate. I wonder why she kept it. I didn't think she even knew I had painted that summer. How strange that she should frame it and keep it here of all places, her private study, a place I always felt was out of bounds. Have I been completely wrong about her?

I decide to stop searching for things I do not understand and leave the study in case I find something else. I am exhausted. I grab my bag from the hall and decide it's time for sleep. I pick the pink room, the one with roses on the wallpaper and a matching bed cover. You could almost call this my room, but I never stayed here long enough to get the sense that it belonged to me. I was always a guest in this house.

The whiskey has made me light-headed and it is as much as I can do to brush my teeth and flop into bed.

The bed is higher than I am used to, and the pillows harder. Despite these unfamiliar surroundings I fall into a deep, deep sleep.

I dream that I am sleeping with my Jack when he is a toddler. His soft curly hair is long and uncut. His cheeks are rosy red from teething. His pyjamas have Barbar the Elephant on them and they are all soft and fleecy. The space between my neck and my right shoulder is the perfect fit for his chubby face. I cuddle him, delighting in his softness, rejoicing in his utter trustfulness, grateful that I have been blessed with this little treasure.

He is asleep but I am not. I am awake and drinking in the warmth of his little body, his perfect form. I am in that tranquil place between love and peace. I am full.

Then, suddenly, the dream changes and Jack is on the forest path to the summer-house. He hasn't got enough clothes on and I am worried he will be cold.

He keeps running ahead of me and hiding behind the bushes. I am nervous. I don't like this game. I can't see him enough. I keep calling him and calling him but he doesn't reappear. Something seems to be holding me back. I can't keep up with him. He is going further and further away. I am screaming for him now and crying. I lose sight of him completely. I begin to panic. Where is he? What should I do?

Should I fetch Charlie? No, no, I must go on and keep looking and keep calling. I can't waste time going back to the main house.

'Jack, Jack, where are you? Mummy's got some chocolate for you; just come out and you can have some chocolate.'

I am running now down the forest path, completely panicked. Then I look up and see him. He's crawling on the forest floor, but no, that's not right, he's crawling on something higher. Dear God, it's the summer-house roof. He's on the roof and he's going to fall all the way down to the river-bed.

Sixty feet at least! I can't stop him. I try to clamber up the drain-pipe at the side of the summer-house but I can't get a good hold and keep slipping. I can see him on the roof and try to coax him to me. He keeps crawling further towards the edge. Something holds me back. I can't get him. What's holding me? Why can't I move?

I turn and see *her* hand on my ankle. She has come out of the summer-house in her nightclothes. She's all thin and frail like she was in the bed but now she's strong too. She won't loosen her grip.

'Let him go, child, let him go,' she says, as I start screaming. I can't shake her off.

It is then that I am aware that I am dreaming. I toss and turn with violence and force myself awake. I sit up with a start and momentarily do not recognize my surroundings. Last night I had forgotten to close the curtains and the room is bathed in morning light. I can see the old grass tennis court from the window and then know where I have slept. I am wet with sweat and shaking. My mouth is dry from the whiskey and I need some water.

Unsteady and unhappy, I make my way downstairs. It's only 6 a.m. by the grandfather clock in the hall. It's too early to ring Karl and see if Jack's all right.

It was only a dream, it was only a dream, I keep telling myself. I pour out a big glass of cold water, drink, and refill it.

I am on my way back upstairs when I hear the phone ring. It takes me a while to find it. It's coming from her study. I pick it up.

'Hello, look, I'm awfully sorry for ringing so early, but could I speak to Helen Rafferty please?' says Karl on the other end.

'Karl it's me, what's the matter?' I ask.

In a strange way I know what's coming. I know from the tone of his voice.

'Helen, it's Jack. Jack's gone missing.'

3

The Note

I DON'T SAY GOODBYE to her. The situation would be too impossible for her to comprehend. I never felt she knew me anyway and now, with her own failing state, it would be beyond expectation that she could be of any practical use or comfort.

A summer storm whips up and rain is pelting down as we leave. Charlie drives me to the train station in the big old estate jeep. The journey is noisy and bumpy. Visibility is restricted, but it doesn't seem to bother him. Normally I would feel at ease in this weather, safeness inside the old battered jeep, but today I am irritated, impatient, on the edge of hysteria.

On the way Charlie keeps shaking his head in disbelief.

'Is there no message, Miss, no reason, why did they pick him?'

'I don't know, I have gone over it again and again in my head and I cannot think why anyone would take a fourteen-year-old boy. The first thought I had was that he had been taken for trafficking but Karl says that doesn't make sense as they didn't even attempt to take the boy who was with him. They knew Jack's name. That frightens me more than anything. He was targeted.'

'And there's no note, no ransom demand?'

'No, not yet. You know that Karl is under investigation, the guards even suspect him.'

'It's a terrible business, Miss.' Charlie keeps repeating. 'It's a terrible business.'

He is visibly upset. I have never seen him this way before. I don't fully understand it. We were never that close. Charlie 'appeared' on the estate after my mother had remarried. He was the farm manager and our paths rarely crossed. Why is Jack's disappearance affecting him so much?

'What will I tell her? What am I going to tell your mother? The shock of it could kill her,' he asks.

Now it hits me. I realize that he is only upset for her; it's nothing to do with me, or Jack, or Karl. My whole world is threatened here. My son, my precious son Jack is gone. It does not even occur to him that for once it's not about her it's about me. Can he not see that?

'Charlie she hasn't even seen Jack for years. What difference is it going to make to her?' I shout. 'Just tell her anything, anything that comes into your head, will you? And get me to the fucking train on time.'

Charlie looks at me coldly. I know my words wound him. Still I am surprised at his retort.

'You're like her, you know, girl? You might try to deny it, but you're cut out of the same cloth.'

Of all the things he could have said this has got to be the worst. For years I have feared that I would become her, that I had some character flaw that would turn me into her. Anger is creeping up in me now. I try to stop it; I know it won't serve any purpose, it won't help Jack, but I have never been good at controlling my emotions.

'Shut up, Charlie, don't ever say that about me. I am *not* like her. Say anything else you like but not that.'

Silence sits between us for a moment; it's a hurt, hard silence. I had wanted to drive myself back in my own car, but Charlie insisted this was the best way. Now I am not so sure.

'Listen you're upset.' he says after a minute, 'so am I, love. I never would have wanted anything like this to happen to you, never would have thought it of ... never would have thought of it.'

There's something curious in the way he says this, but I feel the tears welling up in me and I cannot speak. Why did I ever come back to this place? This place has only ever brought me sadness.

The town is coming into view now. It eases me somewhat to

think that I will soon be on the train, closer to Jack. But there is a queasiness in my stomach that won't go away. It's a nervous, hollow feeling. Where is my Jack? Who has him? What are they doing to him now? Why? I keep asking myself over and over.

Finally we pull up outside the train station and I notice that nothing has changed. It is just how it was when I was a child. We go in to get my ticket and I am transported back to my boarding-school days. I never could understand why I was sent away. Why did she agree to it? I was perfectly happy in the local national school. It was true I was a loner that I didn't have a lot of close schoolfriends, that I would spend hours pored over fantasy books in the local library. Edgar said I would 'integrate' better into the English school system. But when I was sent away it was as if I was being punished. I felt she didn't want me in her new life, that there was no place for me amid the grand rooms of Cillindara.

The platform is still barren and cold. The addition of hanging baskets of summer flowers hasn't helped lift the mood of depression that always overcomes me here.

Charlie insists on buying my ticket and shakes my hand awkwardly as I board the train; it is his attempt at closeness. His eyes are misting over. Maybe I am too hard on him. Perhaps I was too hard on her.

'It'll be all right now, Miss Helen. You have got to be brave. You have been through many a hard time before and got over it. We're all in this together; we'll all be praying for you,' he says, as he leaves me.

'Thanks, thanks, I'll let you know … you know … I'll let you know.' I am choking on my own words as I climb into the carriage. I'll let him know what? That Jack's body could be found dumped somewhere and I'll never see him alive again?

I carelessly throw my stuff onto a seat and sit down. I try hard not to look out the window because I am afraid Charlie will be looking at me and I will start to cry. Eventually I relent and I look up to wave goodbye to him but he's not there. That's odd. I felt sure he would have waited. Where did he rush off to? I leave my seat and get off the train. From the platform I can just about make him out at the station entrance. He's talking to a man who is not familiar. I can only see the stranger's back. I see him grab the man by the shoulders. He is almost shaking him. The train sounds like it is going to start moving and I must go back to my seat. I am left puzzled.

At least the incident makes me more focused. Has Jack's disappearance got something to do with my mother and Charlie, I wonder?

I check my mobile for coverage and am relieved to find it has returned. No point in calling Karl for the umpteenth time this morning. He has the train times. He knows to call as soon as there is a smidgen of information.

The train takes off and picks up speed. I stare out the window, agitated and un-eased. A shiver runs through me even though it is not cold. In what seems like no time a young man in a uniform comes around with a trolley and offers papers and coffee. I am taken aback initially at the unexpected luxuries of first class. I had not even noticed the difference in the carriage. Charlie paid for the ticket. I am not used to that. Money has never come to me easily and I have been cautious with it.

The trolley boy asks what I would like and rather than saying *several valium and a packet of Marlboro Lights* I settle for instant black liquid that presumes to call itself coffee and regretfully obey the no-smoking rule.

I skim through *The Irish Times* looking only at the pictures but wishing I could read in depth so that the time will pass quickly. Concentration is impossible so I stare out the window again but I find the steady motion of the train and the sight of the constant countryside is making me nauseous. I gulp more coffee and in my hurry I spill it so that brown liquid slowly dribbles from the corner of my mouth. I walk to the toilet to splash my face with cold water. I rummage around my bag for some make-up and apply it haphazardly. My appearance is of no consequence, but some sort of activity is vital. As I come out of the toilet I notice that there is a man in-between the carriages. He has the train door window open and is leaning out to smoke. I wonder is that allowed. He makes no gesture to me. There is something familiar about him but I cannot place it. I wander back to my seat, unsettled.

The carriage is almost empty. A woman sits with what looks like two male business colleagues. They are all huddled over a laptop. One of them keeps checking a Blackberry. Their navy pinstripe suits differ ever so slightly. Estate agents for sure, I speculate. They are so easy to spot. I assume they are working on some sort of country land deal. It's common knowledge that there is still money to be made in rural towns.

Edgar and I would always play this game when we were travelling. We would look at strangers and make up their life stories. I always thought I was good at it but of course never find out if I had won. Thoughts of Edgar come back to me, details that I have chosen never to think of, parts of my life that I have ignored.

In my short English school holidays he had always insisted that we travel throughout Europe. We would get the ferry to France and take trains to Paris or Cannes. One year we flew from London to Venice. He was the one who first showed me the Louvre and the Guggenheim, the Eiffel Tower and St Mark's. I used to think that he was trying to replace Julian with me, he paid me such attention.

Julian, poor Julian, lying dead in his grave, his corpse rotting beneath the cold dark earth. I cannot go on if I lose Jack. There will be no future. I force my mind to obliterate that image of Julian and think again about my dying mother. Why did she never come with us on those summer trips? Did they both conspire to keep me away from Cillindara? Both of them would always have some sort of justification for her not coming along: 'she's not well', 'she doesn't like planes', 'she has too much to do on the estate'. Excuses were plentiful but the results left their mark on me; I didn't feel welcome there, a place that should have been my home. A distance grew between myself and her, and I imagined that they both kept me away because I was somehow inadequate, stained in some way. Enough of that now; I chide myself for thinking about my past when my son is missing. But I do have a strong feeling that it is all connected.

I scan the rest of the carriage. Further up a woman sits quietly with a tiny newborn. I don't dwell on her. I cannot be reminded of happy times gone past. Fear for my Jack possesses me. I move on.

Closer to me there is a man, I would say in his late forties. His back is towards me so I cannot see his face. He is wearing a white and red pin-striped business shirt with white collar and cuffs. His suit jacket, navy, made of a lightweight summer cloth, is neatly draped over the table as is his raincoat and a silk paisley scarf. I notice that he has a gold signet ring and an expensive-looking watch on his wrist. Is it a Rolex? I am never any good at recognizing brands. Even so there is money about this man. But as my eyes glance back to his hands, I am slightly surprised. I would have expected them to be manicured, but this man's hands are rough and worn-looking. There is dirt underneath his fingernails. His dark brown-hair is receding and has flecks of grey in it. Maybe he is older than I first thought, but I cannot make out his features from this angle. He is reading a copy of the *Commercial Property* section of the *Irish Independent*. He crosses his legs and I can see his shoes. They are old, scuffed boots. He is a bit of a conundrum then. I look away from him and think that I feel his gaze upon me. Paranoia is rife in my troubled mind.

I sigh at the uselessness of this game, but realize if I stop playing the space in my head will be filled with terrifying thoughts about my Jack.

Close to the man is a middle-aged couple. He is classically hand-some in a Roman kind of way; a well-defined jaw; skin, although aged, is still clear and clean-looking. She is an attractive redhead, well preserved for her age, which I guess is mid-fifties. They are holding hands and smiling at each other. You can see that they are making every attempt at closeness, but must restrain themselves in public. They must be lovers, certainly not married, sneaking away for the day. Why am I so convinced of that? Is it that I believe marriage turns its inhabitants sour and bitter with age as happened with my mother? I look back at the couple and see him kissing her freckled hands. I smile at the thought of their happiness.

I imagine them French kissing and then, unwillingly, my thoughts substitute me and Karl. Immediately I stop because that image doesn't work; it makes me feel uncomfortable. I wonder when we stopped kissing like that.

I think back to when Karl and I first met and remember how confused I was. My life was all change and instability. No home of my own, not one that I wanted to return to in any case, not after that summer. My education had been a disaster and I barely scraped enough A levels to get into art college in Dublin. Mother, of course, was disappointed. 'We should never have sent her away, Edgar. I'm sorry I let you persuade me.' I overheard her say. It was all a little too late for the wayward animal I had become. Once at college I felt disconnected and alone. I knew no one, so initially I had plunged myself into my foundation year working with a manic, feverish enthusiasm. I used pastels, oils and charcoal without restraint. I took little heed of any direction that was offered. I lost myself in my own distractions. Gradually by the end of second year I had amassed a loose collection of friends, mostly through drunken drug-filled parties. I took anything that was going: hash, ecstasy, amphetamines, cocaine and Jack Daniel's. My capacity became legendary. Still there was no anchoring point for me so I worked and partied at a frenzied pace to stop myself from thinking. Then, when Edgar died, I was set adrift completely. I distance myself further from the woman to whom I should have been close. I was afraid of her bitterness, her poisonous tongue, her anger.

That's when I met Karl. He was everything I ever wanted: older, respectable yet still on the edge. I remember feeling that he would save me from myself.

The truth was that the initial passion didn't last long. Over the years the feeling that he was saving me turned full circle and now I feel dragged down by him. I am forever day dreaming of ending it, of leaving him, of starting again with someone else, but there is no one else and I know that I will stay, for Jack I will stay, but what will I do without my Jack?

I begin to cry, quietly, and then berate myself for having so much self-pity. I need to think of Jack and where he is and who has him. What could anyone possibly want with my lovely boy Jack?

My thoughts are interrupted when suddenly there is an announcement that we are approaching Templemore. There is a general shuffling in the carriage and then the ticket inspector arrives. The quietness of the journey is broken and a mood of busyness prevails. The man with the newspaper gets up and gathers his belongings. He puts on thin leather gloves and fixes his scarf casually around his neck and face. That is unusual for the summer. He picks up his coat and drapes it over his arm. When the train slows to a stop he comes towards me. I drop my eyes so that I do not appear to be staring. He passes me and then he stops. His jacket is practically sticking into my face. The coffee cart is on its way back to the buffet car and he motions me to move over while he stands out of its way.

In one swift movement the man lowers himself down to my eye level and puts his mouth close to my ear. His breath smells of last night's whiskey and tobacco. He puts his hand on my neck and jaw so I cannot turn towards him.

His mobile rings. He doesn't answer it.

'I think this call is for you.'

I am confused. My head is immobile so I start a conversation with someone whom I cannot see.

'What, what are you talking about? How could it be for me?' I say, and I try and crane around to see him but his hold is too firm.

'I would urge you to take this call, Mrs Rafferty, before it's too late.'

My God, he knows my name. His grip loosens, the cart has passed. He dumps the mobile on my table along with an envelope and then he disappears down the carriage and out of the train. I see his body shape pass by the window. I don't know whether to go after him, or take the phone or open the envelope. I jump up with the intention of going after him but the ringing mobile is distracting me. I answer it while I am on the move.

'Hello, who is this?'

'Mum, Mum, is that you? … Mum it's me Jack,' says the voice on the other end. I am stunned. I glimpse a view of the man at the end of the platform and think of getting off the train, but when I hear Jack's voice I stop where I am standing.

'Jesus, Jack, where are you? Are you all right?'

'Yes I'm fine, Mum, I'm fine,' Jack says, but I can hear the nervous tone in his voice.

'Tell me where you are, Jack, and I'll come and get you; quick tell me where you are.'

My voice is raised now and the remaining occupants of the carriage have turned around to stare.

'Just do what they say, Mum, OK? Everything will be all right if you do what they say. I love you, Mum, I love …' Click, the call is terminated.

The train starts moving again. I can hardly comprehend that I just spoke to Jack. At least he is alive, I tell myself. My thoughts return to the mystery man. I couldn't see his face. I get up and go to the end of the carriage and look out at the platform. It is empty. Should I get out and try and catch up with him? The train moves off and the decision is made for me. I have left it too late. I am despondent. I return to my seat and notice that the smoker has come into the carriage. He is looking at me. He takes a seat quite close to me. I don't like that.

The envelope is still on my table. I stop shaking enough to open it carefully.

Your father's will is lost. We know that it is hidden in a house that you lived in when you were young. Find it and wait for further instructions. Jack will not be harmed provided you do not contact the police. We repeat, do not involve the police.

I read it over but it makes doesn't make any sense. *My father's will*? Not only do I know nothing about it, but I know practically nothing about my real father. The whole incident has left me panicked.

I glance up and see that the smoker is still looking at me. His manner is restless. He fiddles with his fingernails. It's his jacket; there's something familiar about his jacket. I am just about to make a connection when quite suddenly he changes his seat and comes up to sit right beside me.

'Look, I know you don't know me, Helen but my name is Frank Callan. Charlie sent me.'

Just then I realize that his jacket is the one I saw Charlie shake on the platform.

'Maybe you saw me at the station. Show me the note, Helen. Show it to me.'

4

The Smoker

I DON'T KNOW HOW long it is taking me to stop hyperventilating. This guy Frank is trying to calm me down. The other occupants of the carriage are looking concerned. Frank is telling me quietly that I am in a state of shock. His voice has an incredible calmness that I would not have predicted. He reaches out across the table and holds my hand. His touch is steady, strong and soft all at the same time.

'Settle down, Helen, settle down. Breathe a bit slower or you'll faint. Settle down.'

Slowly my breathing begins to get quiet.

'Let's go to the outside of the carriage and try and discuss what to do from here,' he says.

I go to get up, but realize that I am acting too hastily. How can I trust this man? I am reluctant to move and in any case I doubt the ground will support me if I stand up.

'Look, Frank, I don't know who you are or anything about you. Do you really think I am just going to get up and walk out of this carriage with you? For God's sake, for all I know you could throw me off the bloody train.'

Frank gently lets go of my hand and relaxes back into his seat with a faint smile on his face.

'I'm sorry; of course, I don't know what I was thinking. I'm trying not to create any more alarm. The other passengers are aware that something is up. Can't you see them all looking? I just don't want to attract any more attention. Why don't we get some more coffee and discuss the situation as calmly as we can?'

I stare at him and keep holding on to the note tightly.

'Oh, and by the way, Helen, you do know me; it was so long ago now that you have probably forgotten. But let's forget about that for the moment. Our immediate concern is your son Jack. I saw you get up as if to leave. Then you took a call and read that note. Was there some news of him?'

I consider the cut of Frank before answering. I am still trying to calm down, to think rationally. I have an overwhelming urge to pull the emergency cord and stop the train, to call the police, to talk to Karl, to turn back time, to see Jack smiling, to wake up and find that this awful reality is a nightmare. Something stops me from going into a complete state of panic. An inner voice is telling me to get it together and to take control of the situation. 'Trust your gut, girl, trust your gut', isn't that what Charlie used to always say when I was in trouble?

I survey Frank closely. He has a big build. He's a large man, but not fat. His skin is slightly scarred from acne. His once red hair has flecks of grey in it. His brown eyes stare at me directly with warmth and concern. I can't detect any badness here and, besides, there's a familiarity about him which I can't place. It's more than just seeing the back of him at the train station.

'How do I know you? Give me some reason to trust you. Why should I tell you anything about my son, he is already in danger?'

He pauses and his smile broadens.

'Do you remember that summer you lived on the estate? Do you remember the parties you had in the summer-house?'

'Yes, I remember. Were you at any of them?'

'Oh, I was there all right. There would be a gang of us, myself and, let's say, a lot of hangers on. We were mostly from Quarry Road, you know, up behind the church there? Ring any bells?'

'Yes, yes, I know you now. You guys were wild, seriously wild, always on the edge of trouble.'

He keeps smiling; I find it irritating.

'Frank, this isn't the kind of reassurance I was looking for.'

He sits up and stiffens. His mood is changing.

'Look, Helen, I would love to sit here and tell you my whole fucking life story, but try to believe me, I am acting in your best interests. Time is running away with us. Charlie trusts me and you trust Charlie, don't you? That's the only damn reassurance I can give you. Take it or leave it. I can get off at the next stop and you can sit here stewing over that note on your own, or you can take a chance with me. Which is it?'

In any other circumstances, I would be more cautious, but I am confused. That note has my head spinning. It's another hour and half on the train to Dublin and I don't feel that I have much choice.

'Yes, OK, I'm going to have to go with you, I suppose.'

'Right, let's go over the conservation you had with the man for starters, and show me that piece of paper you're holding on to so tightly.'

After I have filled him in, he suggests I check the mobile. As is expected there is no call history on it, no number ID of the call received and no names in the data base. We conclude it's a new pay as you go phone. Our attention turns to the note. He examines it closely. It's on standard A4 white paper, printed off in Arial script.

Your father's will is lost. We know that it is hidden in a house that you lived in when you were young. Find it and wait for further instructions. Jack will not be harmed provided you do not contact the police. We repeat, do not involve the police.

'Do you know anything about your father's will, Helen?'

'Frank, I don't even know anything about my father.'

'But, Helen, wasn't your father Edgar Royston?'

'No, he was my stepfather.'

Frank is very surprised.

'Really, I never knew that. I always presumed that Mr Royston was your father.'

'Well he wasn't, all right? Don't you think that I know who my own father was?'

There is an embarrassing silence. I can feel myself redden.

'Daniel Fitzgerald was my father, for your information,' I say after a few minutes. 'He came from my mother's home town. He died in America before I was born though, so I actually don't know a lot about him.'

He eases back in his seat again, fingering the note, looking puzzled. He straightens his posture.

'OK let's go through the note again … "*hidden in a house that you lived in when you were young*". Where did you live when you were young, Helen?'

'I came to the village of Cillindara when I was about four years old.'

'But you didn't live in Cillindara House initially?'

'No; before my mother married Edgar Royston we lived in the village, beside the bakery, on Hill Street. Do you know it?'

'Sure, wasn't I brought up nicking fairy-cakes from your woman, old Mrs Bates?' I smile at the thought of Mrs Bates in her apron shooing young lads out of her shop. 'They are a row of terraced houses aren't they?'

His familiarity with the village immediately makes me feel more comfortable.

'Yes, yes, that's right, little terraced houses.'

'How long did you live there?'

'Till I was twelve. Then she remarried and that's when I was sent away to boarding-school.'

I try to hide any remnants of bitterness in the tone of my voice but I am not sure if I succeed. He doesn't seem to notice and continues his barrage of questions.

'So it could be there, or it could be Cillindara House.'

'It's not likely to be Cillindara House. I never really lived there, only for a couple of weeks here and there on holidays. I didn't even spend my summers there most of the time.'

'Really, why not?'

I don't want to go into this with Frank.

'I just didn't. Edgar, my stepfather, and I travelled to Europe on school holidays.'

'Where were you at school, some fancy place in England?'

I think this man knows too much about me.

'Various boarding-schools. I didn't stay longer than two years in any of them.'

He looks at me quizzically. I am not about to give him chapter and verse on the number of times I was expelled. I haven't quite made up my mind about how much he needs to know.

'That doesn't help us then. Tell me, Helen, where would you have considered home when you were young?'

'Hill Street I suppose. After that there was nothing but a series of boarding-schools and then I rented and shared houses at college before I bought my own home.'

I can see that he is as confused about the note as I am.

'Where did you live before – before you came to the village?'

'I don't know exactly. My mother told me I lived in her home place in Kerry, but I have never been there. I couldn't even pick it out on a map.'

'Was it with your mother or your father's family? What's the name of the place? Do you remember anything about it? Come on, Helen, you must know something. Think back, think back.'

I have tried to remember life before Cillindara but it's too long ago, I have no picture of it. There is more silence. I am lost in my own scrambled thoughts. Too many things are going on in my head and I cannot think clearly. I am in overload. Frank shuffles about in his seat. He softens.

'I'm sorry if I'm going a bit heavy on you, Helen. I'm just concerned that's all. I'm going to get us a coffee – how do you take yours?'

'Black, strong and sugared.'

He smiles again. 'Same as the old days.'

How could he have remembered, I wonder?

'Try to gather your thoughts while I am gone. You are the key to whatever is going on here. My hunch is that we will just have to turn around and go back down to Cillindara as soon as we hit Dublin. We have to touch base with Karl though and get him out from under police suspicion. I'll be back as soon as I can.'

Frank gets up slowly and, as he exits the carriage, I see for the first time that he has a noticeable limp. It's on his left side. He goes awkwardly through the carriage door and disappears. My head falls between my hands as I try desperately to assess the situation.

I remember evenings with my mother in Hill Street when I was small. When I started school I became aware that other children had fathers and I didn't. I knew mine was dead but naturally I was curious.

'What was my daddy like, Mama?'

'Like you pet, just like you,' she would say softly.

'Can we go and visit him like we visit Mr Royston's boy in his grave?'

'No, Helen, it's too far away. Your Daddy is buried all the way across the sea in America. Maybe when you're bigger, pet. Go on with you now, Helen, you can see I'm busy.' And she would just go on working on the accounts for the Royston business.

As I got older I wanted more details: a photograph, a story from his childhood, information on his brothers and sisters. But she never gave me any real information. The harder I pressed the more evasive she became. Any time I brought the subject up she had a way of pursing her lips so I knew that she was angry. I was never going to get any answers so I stopped asking. Why was she so reticent about him?

I repeat the words of the note again to myself: *A house that you lived in when you were young.*

I close my eyes and make my mind go blank. It takes a few moments to rid myself of random thoughts. With huge effort I transport myself back to the time before I came to Cillindara village. I think I have a memory of before I was four although I can't be sure if it's a real memory, or if I just made it up. I can see a woman in black sitting beside a turf fire. If I try very hard I think I can feel the heat of it. The woman is thin and her face is very creased. She is knitting. I am sitting on a cold, flagstone floor beside her helping her with the wool. Was she my granny? Was I in my father's house? I lose my concentration and the image of the old woman disappears into some far off corner of my mind only to be replaced with my Jack's face. My frustration with the note is palpable. I feel powerless.

I make myself think of something more practical than a murky memory and I think of Charlie. He must know more about my father than he has ever told me. Sure, wasn't he talking about him last night in the kitchen? I am amazed that I have lived my life with such blindness of my own roots. I could have explored it when I became an adult. It was never a topic of conversation. Goodness knows I had to sit through a lot of boring speeches by Edgar Royston about the importance of the family line; about how the Roystons had lasted six generations on the same land. He insisted that I knew the names of all his ancestors; he pored over old photographs with me, discussed the setting up of the family firm. It is preposterous that I know so much about my stepfather's family and so little about my own.

Why did I never probe deeper into my own father's family, my mother's? I had adored my mother when I was younger. She was as beautiful as a fairy princess and I wished and wished that a handsome prince would come along and rescue her from our mean little life in Hill Street. But I should have been more careful about what I wished for. Things began to change as soon as she and Edgar became involved and I took second place in her life. I don't know whether I started hating her first or she me. What does it matter? I hated her enough to stay away from her all these years. I hated her enough to never bother finding out who she really was. I hated her enough to be left with this incomprehensible useless note that won't bring Jack back.

I reflect on my conversation in the car with Charlie on the way to the station. Was he hiding something? Why would anyone take Jack, why?

I decide to ring him from my mobile. He answers the house phone after one ring. He must have been sitting by it.

'Charlie, it's me, Helen.'

'Yes I know, *a stór*. Have they found Jack? Did he turn up somewhere? Has Frank got you yet?'

'No, Charlie, he has not been found and, yes, Frank has made contact.'

'You can trust him, Helen. He's a good lad.'

'Are you sure about him, Charlie? He knows a lot about me.'

'I am dead certain, girl, that Frank Callan will help you out. You can be sure of it.'

The conviction in his words is reassuring.

'Thanks, Charlie. I got a note, and I need you to tell me about my father, Daniel Fitzgerald.'

I fill him in on the developments so far. Charlie says he has no idea who the man on the train is, nor does he know any details about a will. He agrees to search my mother's study and the whole house in an attempt to uncover any hidden wills, or other legal documents that might be important. He keeps telling me how my mother is failing today and how I have to get back down to Cillindara as soon as this is all over.

I can't think that far ahead. Every second of my existence is tied up with the idea of getting Jack back. I can't waste any energy thinking about her. That will have to do for later.

I keep pressing him.

'Right, Charlie, but what about her and Daniel?'

'It's just as I was telling you last night, girl, Daniel and I were very fond of her, she was a real beauty your mother. Sometimes she'd come to dances with us, just local hops, and we would walk her home, together. I always felt I never would have had a chance with her. I thought Daniel felt the same way. Do you know what I am saying, Helen?'

'Yes I do, Charlie, I do.' And I think that what he really means is that she considered herself a bit above them. I can imagine that being the truth of it, but Charlie can't say it like that. I think about the way she treated him on the estate in Cillindara, an employee, not a childhood friend.

'Me and Daniel headed off for America. My brothers had gone ahead of me and we went after them. There was nothing in Kerry for us at that time.'

'But Charlie, what about Daniel and my mother? Weren't they married? Why did she not go with you?'

Charlie hesitates. 'There was some talk of her following on when we got set up but it didn't turn out like that.'

'What happened then?'

'I know this might upset you, Helen, but, but ...'

'But what? There's no time to hide anything now, tell me everything please.'

'You see, Daniel and your mother weren't married, Helen. I didn't even know they had ... you know ... had intentions like, let alone ... let alone ...'

'You mean you didn't know she was pregnant when you left for America? Is that what you are saying?'

'Yes that's it; I didn't know about it at all.'

'Then why did she always claim she was married to him?'

'She only claimed to be a widow when she moved to Cillindara, Helen. In her own village, she was – she was marked as an unmarried mother. You must remember the times back then, Helen. You were born in 1969. I can remember hearing about your birth from a relative back home. The parts of Kerry we came from, well, the people were still under the thumb of the Catholic Church. It was different times back then.'

'And Daniel, he was definitely my father?'

'That is what she claimed in Donntra. When I came back from America that was what I always supposed was the truth. That's all I knew about it. I never questioned it.'

'Didn't you ask though, ask Daniel outright about it? Did he know about me?'

'I never got a chance to find out, unfortunately. You see we fell out when we got to America, me and Daniel. I argued with him about some girl in a bar. One of those stupid drunken fights you have when you're young lads and suddenly it went the wrong way. We were hurling insults at each other and it ended up in a brawl. We never made up after it. I didn't see him for a couple of months and then I heard, from one of my brothers, that he had fallen off some scaffolding on a construction job on the Upper East Side. He was on the twenty-first floor with no safety harness. He had the streak of a gambler in him, Daniel; he always took risks. He usually got away with it but this was one risk too many for him. I heard of it too late to attend the funeral. I was sorry then, of course; sorry that I didn't remain friends with him to the end.'

'So he's dead then, Charlie; he's been dead a long time but did anyone go to his funeral? What proof is there that he is dead?'

'Look he never turned up again, Helen, so for me, that is good enough proof. We would have heard something from somewhere. He had no reason to disappear. I'm sure he would have gone back and married your mother as soon as he heard about you.'

'All right Charlie, that's enough for now I suppose. I have to think about what you have said. It's a lot to take in. I'll talk to you when I get to Dublin.'

I let go of the conversation reluctantly. There are so many more things I need to know, but not now. Now I have to read the ransom note again and try and make more sense of it.

I search around for it, but it is nowhere on the carriage seat or table. Frank should be back by now. I am getting nervous. Did he take the note with him?

I decide to go in the general direction of the dining-car, full sure I will run into him on the way. But it doesn't happen. I slow down as I near it. I begin to check the occupants of the seats. How could I have missed him? The dining-car is largely empty, except for a few stragglers having the last of the breakfast. I remember I haven't eaten and wonder whether to stay here, eat and wait, or go back down to my original seat. The thought of food turns my stomach. I choose to retrace my steps, slower this time, wondering did I miss him when he was leaning out of a window, smoking? I begin to doubt my own judgement. How did he know so much about me? Maybe some of it came from local gossip, but I can't be sure. Anyway, I think with a start, how did he know about Karl being under police suspicion? I didn't tell him. Did Charlie fill him in on everything? I start getting anxious when I still can't see him. I am just about to re-enter my carriage again when Frank appears from an alcove near the outside door. Quite suddenly he pulls me towards him and holds me in an embrace that indicates we are closer than new acquaintances. He gestures to stay quiet, looks me straight in the eyes, and whispers, 'There's a guy in the carriage begging. I watched him work the train. For some reason when he got to your seat he left a note on your table. See him?'

He swings me round and I glimpse a view of a thin, scrawny teenager in baggy jeans and trainers. There is belligerence in his stance. He's dawdling at the back of the carriage.

'He waited for you to go past him in the next car before he made his move. I stayed behind to watch and he hasn't seen me. I'm getting ready to corner him if he comes past, but the train is stopping in two minutes for Portarlington. I suggest you go back and read the note. If he gets out at the next stop be ready to get out too. I'll jump and tail him. You'll have to catch up. OK, you got all that, Helen?'

'Yes, yes, Frank, I've got it.'

5

The Jump

THE TWO-MINUTE JOURNEY to Portarlington seems to take forever. I make my way back through the carriage and can feel Frank's eyes on me from the back and the unknown teenager from the front. Unsteady, I adjust to the slowing of the train and then plonk back into my seat. I immediately grab the folded-up piece of paper. It is worn. In carefully written childish block capitals it reads:

I HAVE SOMETHING FOR YOU BUT I NEED MONEY FIRST.

I am confused. What is this new twist? What could this boy possibly know?

I look up and see that the boy is staring at me from the back of the carriage. I nod to him in acknowledgement and he makes to come towards me. As he does so the train slows and enters a tunnel. The carriage is suddenly darkened. The train lurches and I see a shape, which I presume is the boy's, stumble. Another shape, it must be Frank, appears from behind me. The tunnel and the darkness seem to go on forever. The shapes get mingled up and move away from me.

Light blasts back into the carriage and the train stops at the station. I can see no boy and no Frank. I cannot work out what has happened or where they have gone.

In a panic, I run and check both ends of the carriage. There is no sign of them. What am I to do?

I look out and check the platform. About twenty people have got off and are clustering around the exit gate. I check the carriage ends again but to no avail. I have no choice but to get off the train. I hurriedly assemble my belongings. Instinctively, I start running up the platform as the small crowd at the exit diminishes and scatters. As I catch up I cannot see Frank or the boy. They couldn't have gone that fast. I scan the station entrance. No sign. I run out of the station and look up and down the street. There is still no clue. I rush back into the station. I see the train timetable. The next one to Dublin is not for another hour. There is nothing going back to Cillindara for two hours. The train sounds like it's about to start up again.

I have no idea what to do. I see a man come out from the men's toilets. He looks perturbed, as if he has seen something unpleasant. I decide to have a look. I take a deep breath and walk straight past the swing door marked *Fir*. The urinals are empty. The floor is wet with a mixture of water and urine. The smell is overpowering. All the cubicles are open. There is a kind of groaning coming out of one of them.

'Frank, Frank, is that you? The train is about to leave. We have to get back on to make Dublin. Frank?'

I am almost shouting with panic as I approach the furthest door. Then, I see a man sitting on a toilet seat; he looks unhealthily thin, only wearing a string vest and jeans. Faded tattoos cover his arms. There's a rubber band around one of them. In between his teeth he's holding a syringe. He's about to shoot up.

'Fancy a hit, missus? I'll do you one for a score,' he says, and looks at me with the familiar addict's hollow eyes.

Oh no, not again. I am not going here. I turn away with a mixture of disgust and empathy. I start running out of the toilets.

Unnerved now, I am back on the main platform. I can see the train is starting to move. I think about jumping on but all the carriage doors are closed except the second to last one, the one where Frank is. The door is open and he is hanging out, motioning to me with one arm.

'Come on, Helen, come on,' he's shouting.

He draws the attention of the guard who stands at the ticket gate. The guard is between me and the carriage. If I wait where I am the train will be moving too fast by the time it gets to me. I break into a sprint. The guard tries to stop me, but I am too agile for him. I skip past him. Good practice from my running away days. I am bolting to the open carriage door. Frank leans out this time with two hands. Someone is holding onto his legs, so he is anchored. I trust him. I jump.

For a minute I go completely blank. Time stands still as I leap into midair and pray that I have done it right. What if I fall? What happens if I end up a mangled wreck in-between the train and the track? I remember a time when I wouldn't have cared, but not now, for my Jack, I have to get it exact.

Frank and I judge it right. He grabs me and, with an incredible shunt, we both fall backwards, landing on the boy who has obviously been holding onto his legs. The relief of it all makes me start laughing. In between bursts of uncontrollable hysterics I manage to tell Frank about my experience in the gents' toilet. He tells me he was stuck in the train loo with 'our young friend'. We all begin to laugh now together, the noise gathering a frantic pitch.

It seems ridiculous. Less than two days ago I had my ordinary quiet life, my son, my business, my order. Now my Jack is missing and I'm laughing hysterically with a man I have just met and a strange teenager. The laughter is in danger of turning.

6

The Card

WE BEGIN TO REASSEMBLE ourselves and decide to retreat to the dining car. I notice Frank has a tight grip on the young guy's arm. He leads the way. The boy begrudgingly introduces himself as Derek. He has longish unbrushed brown hair that falls into his eyes. He has a scar on his left cheek. It looks like a knife wound. He has a thick Dublin accent. I am wary of him.

As we settle at a table a steward takes our order.

'Nice jump there, miss,' says the steward. 'We were cheering for you down the back. You made a right eejit out of that guard.'

'So I did.'

'Jesus, I'm sorry about all of that, Helen. I was *detained* here with Derek and couldn't warn you to stay on the train. You're a damn fast sprinter though, I'll give you that. It would have been an awful mess if you hadn't got back on. Sure, I don't even know where you live in Dublin, never mind what Karl looks like.'

'Yes, I was getting to that, I—'

But he interrupts before I can quiz him on how he knows about Karl.

'Helen, listen. Derek was telling me that he has something for you. He says that he saw the man talking to you on the train and that he dropped this "item" on his way off. Derek thinks it may be of interest to you.'

'Oh, is that what he says? But, Frank, he wasn't even in the last carriage at the time. How does he know I would be interested in what the man dropped?'

'That's exactly what I thought myself, but I haven't been able to get anything else out of him except that this is not a free service he's offering.'

I look now at Derek, closely. Frank and I are talking as if he is not here. It doesn't seem to disturb him. Coffee and sandwiches arrive. Derek opens up one of the sandwiches and starts packing the contents into his mouth and gulping coffee to wash it down.

'OK, Derek, you are claiming that the man dropped something and that you want to sell it to me. Is that it?'

'That's righ'.'

'How did you see this man talk to me? You weren't even in the carriage at the time.'

'I was comin' out of the toilet and checking out first-class at the same time.'

'Checking out first-class? Are you a thief, Derek?'

'Who said anyt'ing 'bout bein' a thief? I'm just doing you a favour that's all.'

'How could you tell, Derek, just from the fact that I was talking to that man, that I would want anything of his?'

'I just knew it, OK? Now, do youse want it or not? It'll cost a ton.'

'I don't believe you, Derek. How did you know I would be interested in anything that man had?'

'I saw youse talking, didn't I? He had your neck in a grip, didn't he? You went all white after he left and then he shot out of the train and hoofed it out of the station. I'm not stupit, you know.'

Frank and I look at each other questioningly. I suppose it could be true. I was attracting attention when I got the phone call and the note. I decide that whatever the information is, it's more important than this boy's version of how he got it.

'Hand it over then, Derek, for God's sake, whatever it is and however you got it. Hand it over,' I bark.

Derek stares at me with no emotion. It seems he is used to people speaking to him this way. It doesn't bother him. He takes a sip of his coffee and savours it. I want to lean over the table, grab him by the collar, and shake him.

Then I notice how young he is, maybe 16 or 17. He is not much older than my Jack. I wonder where his mother is. I don't want anyone to speak to Jack like I speak to him. I change tack.

'Derek, my son is in danger. He is missing; he is all alone and I have to help him. If you give me whatever it is that you have it could help me to find him. Please, Derek, please.'

'Now look here, I don't now anythin' 'bout that.'

'I'm glad you told us that, Derek,' interjects Frank, 'because I have a couple of friends in the guards who might be very interested in talking to you when we get to Dublin.'

Derek hesitates and begins to get irritated. He is a bit fazed by the mention of the guards.

'Look, I've told youse I know nothing about that. Now, are you paying or not? Youse have nothin' on me.'

He rubs his fingers together indicating again he wants to get paid.

'Derek, how much? How much do you want?'

'A ton. I told youse,' he says.

I look confused.

'That's a hundred euros to you.'

'All right, you can have it,' I say, and I dig into my wallet and retrieve two €50 notes. He takes them and examines them carefully against the light from the window as if in some way this will verify their authenticity. When he is satisfied he slowly puts his hand down his trousers and shuffles around in his seat.

Frank raises his eyes to heaven.

'It's no wonder I couldn't find it,' he mutters.

Derek pulls out a business card. It's embossed. It belongs to a solicitor.

> *Joseph Hayes Cunningham*
> *Montenotte House*
> *28 Fitzwilliam Square*
> *Dublin 2*

On the back of the card in an untidy handwritten scrawl are the words:

Ballytain, Co. Kerry.

I show it to Frank and we take turns to stare at it. I keep focusing on the business card. A solicitor, what could he have to do with it? Was the man who gave me the note on the train this solicitor, or is this just one of his contacts? Joe Hayes, Joseph Cunningham, Hayes Cunningham, I keep changing the order around in my head to see if it will mean anything. Nothing; nothing comes.

Montenotte House

It is definitely odd that I had a conversation with Charlie about my mother working for legal people in Montenotte and now the same name is mentioned, albeit for an address in Dublin.

Then the address on the back.

Ballytain, Co. Kerry

Ballytain I have never heard of before. My mother, I know, comes from Kerry and Charlie mentioned Donntra, but I don't know its exact geographical location and have no idea where Ballytain is. Still, it is a link and further convinces me that Jack's disappearance has something to do with my mother and my real father.

'Well, any clues?' says Frank, after a few minutes.

I explain the tenuous connection to Frank.

'It's a lead, if nothing else. We can work on it as soon as we get up to speed with Karl in Dublin. I know a good few legals; one of them will know something about Hayes Cunningham. It's a good result, Helen, don't look so down about it.' He starts talking to Derek but I don't seem to hear. Their speech becomes a muffled mumble of nonsensical words.

I sit and stare at the business card. I start thinking again. I close my eyes to concentrate on a past that I have tried so long to forget. I buried things deeply, so deep that sometimes I don't know if incidents I remember actually happened, or if I just made them up. Occasionally people remind me of some event long ago that seems to be completely wiped from my memory. Yet I can remember trivia, and details about the smallest things: the colour of my shoelaces when I was seven; my school concert when I was ten; the pink hair slide Mother gave me when I went to boarding-school; the price of the butterfly cakes at the bakery; the ticking clock in the hall of Hill Street; the first time I saw my mother kiss Edgar. Why is that I wonder?

I try to concentrate on my childhood days but my mind is wandering again. However much I try, my thoughts keep going back to the time when I first brought Jack down to see *her*. I was driving a beaten-up old Volvo and I was lucky to make it all the way down to Cillindara in one piece. I was so nervous and wanted to have everything right. I made sure Jack was in his best baby clothes: little red and white striped dungarees from Gap, a snow-white t-shirt. The outfit lasted all of twenty minutes. After the first bottle of formula he threw up all over himself.

I stopped at a petrol station and changed him into his second-best outfit, chiding myself all the time for being so stupid as to not leave him in his pyjamas until we had got nearer the town. He was not used to long car journeys. I didn't think of that. I had only stopped breast feeding him a couple of days before and he had not gotten used to formula. I could not face the thought of breastfeeding in front of my mother. I knew she would hate it. He threw up again just as we pulled up outside the big gates of the estate. This time not so badly. I did my best to mop it up with baby wipes and while he didn't look too bad you could smell the vomit from his clothes. I didn't want this. I wanted to arrive with my lovely, shining boy, happy and proud. Now it wasn't going to happen.

She was all smiles at the door, greeting the return of the prodigal daughter and her only grandchild. I was flustered. It didn't take her long to detect the sick and turn.

'Have you no change of clothes for him? Really, Helen, how could you do that to the child? You must always bring a change of clothes wherever you go. Now bring him upstairs straightaway and pop him into the bath.'

'But Mother I did have—' But she cut me off, not listening to me long enough to hear my excuses.

'Mrs Molloy will bring you up some fresh clothes that *I* bought for him.'

The visit was testy and fractious after that. The clothes I had to put Jack in were like a strait jacket; a stiff, starched white shirt with ridiculous lace around the collar that irritated his soft skin, velvet trousers that had to be dry cleaned after every wear.

He acted up horribly and he never normally did that with me. He sensed my mood. He was still at that age where he could not separate his identity from mine. I could not wait to get out of there. She started drinking before lunch; gin and tonics as an aperitif, white wine when the food arrived. With each sip of alcohol her remarks got more caustic, more hurtful. 'You'd think the boy's father could buy you a decent car. That thing looks like it's going to blow a gasket any minute.' I made up some spurious excuse and left early. She said goodbye with a mixture of pity and disdain, insisting on stuffing a £(IR)50 note into Jack's little fist. 'It was always our way in the country,' she explains. It was unusual for her to even mention that. I got as far as the big iron gates when I saw Mrs Molloy running up behind the car. She handed me Jack's sick clothes which she had washed and dried. She saw I was upset.

'She doesn't mean it, miss, you know she doesn't mean it,' is all she could say.

As soon as I was out the gate I burst into floods of uncontrollable sobbing.

'Where are you, Helen?' I can hear Frank asking and my thoughts jump quickly back to the present.

'Oh, just somewhere back.'

'We're in Dublin now.'

As we get off the train Derek continues to tag along. The three of us reach the end of the platform and Frank slows. He sees Karl and looks surprised.

'That your fella there, is it, Helen, the guy with the grey hair?'

'That's not my fella, Frank, that's my husband and you don't have to hide your surprise: I know he looks old enough to be my father.'

7

The Business

KARL GIVES US A small nod of recognition as we approach the end of the platform. He looks polished as usual. He is wearing his signature white, loose weave, cotton shirt, beige chinos and crumpled off-white linen jacket. His grey hair, thinning, is slicked back. The lines on his face add a deceptive air of refinement. His blue eyes are vacant and cold, always so hard to read. He gives me a stiff hug. He stands back immediately after making contact as if to rid himself of my fleeting touch. It's as if I contaminate him in some way. That's how it is with him now. I had forgotten momentarily.

'Helen, how are you?' he asks

'I'm terrible, what would you expect Karl?'

'Yes, of course, that is to be expected,' he agrees.

He turns to Frank and they briefly introduce themselves. 'Charlie told me there would be someone with you.'

I am relieved at this anyway as it saves me the convoluted explanation of how I ended up with a stranger on the train.

Derek takes on a hunted look. His eyes don't meet Karl's. There are no introductions for him. Karl glares at him unkindly and Derek, as if sensing the immediate disapproval, takes a step away from him. There is a short exchange between Derek and Frank where they seem to swap numbers, then Derek goes to disappear into the crowd. Suddenly I run to him and go to shake his hand but it ends up in an awkward hug.

'Goodbye, Derek, and thanks for your help. Take care of yourself now, won't you?' He smiles, embarrassed by my concern. Then he vanishes into the throng of people at the station. Karl gives me a look of displeasure and disdain. I shouldn't expect him to understand.

The three of us make our way to Karl's car. Frank stays a couple of steps behind and makes a call.

'Are you sure this chap is bona fide?' Karl asks, as those blue eyes go towards Frank and he pulls a little too hard on my arm.

'Look, Charlie rang you about him, didn't he?'

'Yes.'

'He helped me on the train.'

'What do you mean "helped you"? Why did you need help?'

'I'll explain in the car, Karl; for the moment I think we should go with him.'

'He's coming with us then?'

'Yes, yes, of course.'

Karl raises his eyes to heaven, the familiar sign of disapproval. As we approach his old Jaguar, Frank catches up.

I get into the back and leave Frank the front seat. 'Tell me again, right from the beginning, Karl, I want to go over every detail,' I say, as soon as we are all in.

'Look, Helen, stop torturing yourself. I told you the story at least three times since this morning. Magda and her boy are back at our house. It's better you hear it from him first hand. He's the only witness anyway.'

It irritates me that he can't refer to my best friend's son by his Christian name. Tommy has been coming in and out of our house for years. There is no point in picking him up on it now. It's just a clear indication of how little regard he has for anyone but himself.

'What about the guards? What are they doing?'

'Very little at the moment, given the circumstances of Jack's disappearance. They think he might turn up somewhere. They are waiting to talk to you as well. At first they didn't take it seriously at all. They thought this was fairly usual behaviour for a boy of his age. Then a couple of detectives got involved and they started asking all sorts of questions about me, as if I'd have an ulterior motive. They wanted to know if there was any trouble at home, marital problems, that sort of thing. They were suspicious and accusatory in their tone; completely off the mark.'

I wonder what he told them. Did he paint a picture of a normal, happy South County Dublin family? Did he keep up the pretence that we both know is a complete farce?

'And now?'

'Well, I'm in the clear naturally enough. I was highly surprised that they grilled me on everything about the gallery and my business interests instead of concentrating their resources on looking for Jack.'

'Why were they so interested in the gallery?'

'I have absolutely no idea. There's nothing to report there, Helen, you know that,' he snaps.

I can sense that he is not at ease talking about his business in front of Frank. I don't feel the slightest bit of sympathy for him. I have long suspected that he does not run a completely legitimate operation. I never did completely comprehend the intricacies of the art world in any case and his involvement in it made me slightly jealous. I suppose I had imagined that I would be a famous painter one day but I had to abandon that ambition when Jack was born. I dropped out of art college and concentrated on making money instead. Painting wasn't going to provide a home for us. But it had wounded me and I viewed Karl's continued involvement in the art business as an indulgent luxury.

'I've been up most of the night talking my way out of the accusation that I kidnapped my own son. It's ridiculous,' he continues.

'When did you report him missing?'

'At nine o'clock last night, or thereabouts,' he mutters. 'The thing is without a ransom demand of any kind the guards don't have much to go on, do they?'

'Sorry, Karl, I should have told you immediately – there is a ransom note but we don't understand it.'

'We?'

I explain the events on the train to him. I hand him the note and the business card when we are stopped in traffic.

Karl is shocked. I can see the colour drain from his face. Some part of him probably did believe the guards' initial assumption that Jack had gone off on a jaunt around the country. The production of the ransom note makes it clear that Jack really was taken. This is a definite orchestrated kidnapping.

'You mean that little scutty guy who came off the train with you had the card? Why did you let him go like that? He could be part of all this. We should have turned him over to the guards immediately.'

'Look, I spoke to him for half an hour on the train,' Frank interjects. 'He's just an innocent. I'm pretty sure he didn't know any more than he was telling us. I think I've got him covered. He's going to ask on the street for us on a pay to know basis. He could be more useful to us that way.'

'Anyway, we don't know if this solicitor or the scrawl on the back of the card has anything to do with it. Frank is going to make a few calls as soon as we get back to our house and see what we can find out about Hayes Cunningham,' I add quickly, but I can sense the tension building up in the car.

'*Oh, is he?*' says Karl. 'I would have thought that I'd have some say in how we are going to proceed from here seeing as it's *my* son that's missing Helen.'

Blood rushes to my face and I can feel myself getting ready for yet another shouting match with Karl. I am saved by Frank.

'The card the young fella gave us could be entirely irrelevant. It's just something to start on. I know a lot of people who could make enquiries on our behalf, discreetly like.'

That's it, Karl is about to blow.

'Frank, before we go any further I'd like to know who the hell you really are. You may be a friend of Charlie's and Helen certainly seems to trust you, but I, personally, would like to know who is privy to confidential information about my son particularly given the severity of the situation that he is in.'

'Fair enough, I agree with you entirely. I am getting so carried away with the urgency of the situation that I have forgotten my manners. Let me explain: my name is Frank Callan. I'm in the building game. I have my own company. Helen's mother and Charlie did me a few favours when I was starting off. They were very kind to me as a matter of fact.'

This news hits me like a sledgehammer – my mother doing someone a favour? It doesn't seem like her style.

'OK, Frank, but why are you getting involved in all of this? This is certainly not your area,' I ask.

'It's like this Helen.' And I notice that he directs all his conversation to me and none at all at Karl. He swivels right around in the front seat to turn and face me.

'I have always believed in returning favours. I rang the main house this morning to enquire after your mother and Charlie filled me in on what happened to your boy. I just want to make myself available to you in any capacity you see fit. If finance becomes an issue, for example, I can provide cash easily. You may need me so I just think I should stick around. Of course, if you want me to bow out at this stage I will go right away. It's whatever you see fit.'

'That's very good of you,' I say, and I must admit to feeling warm towards Frank. He's easy going and calm in a potentially hysterical situation. He's a buffer between me and Karl. Yes, I would like him to stay.

'By the way what's the name of your company?'

'Shandon Enterprises.'

Jesus, they are a huge company. Now I realize who Frank Callan really is. No wonder he's so familiar. I've seen his picture in the papers lots of times. He is usually at the launch of some big residential housing scheme or quoted in the *Irish Times* Property Supplement. He is far more successful than his appearance portrays.

'I set up Shandon in the nineties,' he continues. 'All in all I make a few quid.' And he gives me a wink as he says it. 'I believe you're involved in the property game yourself, Helen.'

'Oh, me? Yes, bits and pieces. You know, nothing big, not in your league anyway,' I reply.

I wonder again how he knows so much about me. But how much does he really know? He knows only what people can see from the outside. What would he say if I told him that I have spent the last ten years embroiled and obsessed with the property game? As I look back I realize that my pattern hasn't changed since art college. I bought my first house for £(IR)130,000 back in '95. Karl had given me the money for the deposit and I had gone through all sorts of hoops with the bank to get the rest. I put forty grand into it and sold it for £(IR)250,000 a year later. On the strength of that I borrowed more and bought more property. Buy, do up and sell or, buy, rent and sell or, best bet: buy, do nothing at all and sell. It was easy to make money on a rising tide. With each sale I had more equity and could finance bigger purchases with bigger profit potential. I could diversify. It became my business and a bloody good one it was too. I needed the money to support myself and my son. Karl contributed sporadically and I hated him for that, for leaving me in constant uncertainty. But in truth it became a greedy life. I could never own enough and once I got a feel for it, property became an obsession. I look back on my life over the last number of years and instead of being happy with what I had I let the obsession take over. There's been endless examination of property supplements in every broadsheet, poring over annual estate agents' reports. I carry around an encyclopaedic knowledge in my head of prices achieved at auction; know every street in my area; can guess the correct layout of each house before I even view it – pre-war bungalows, 1970s three-bedroom semis, two up and two downs, Edwardian red-brick terraces, single-storey over basement villas, two-storey Victorians with returns and garden levels, they're all the same to me once I can identify the type. I have the ability to walk into a house and immediately assess its potential, working out the orientation of the site in my head, knocking down walls in my imagination, furnishing rooms with white couches and silk curtains. The thrill of knowing when a place is just right and I have to have it. Throwing down deposits on new developments is like throwing down dice in a game of snakes and ladders. The buzz of the auction room, the excitement of the bidding, the exhilaration when I sign the contract and know that it is mine. I have been truly possessed. And to what end? None of it matters if I lose the only person that I have ever truly loved: my son Jack.

Karl is still annoyed. He doesn't verbally concede that it's all right for Frank to hang around but his silence indicates some sort of acceptance. I suppose it would have been better for him if Frank had turned out to be some lackey from the estate. I don't think he was expecting Frank to stand his ground.

The atmosphere is, nevertheless, uneasy. The rest of the trip is made in stilted attempts at conversation. I can hear them begin to talk about the legal profession and I switch off.

The leather seats are getting unbearably hot in the May sun. I have to wind the window all the way down. The fumes from a bus beside us are nauseating. I just want to get home.

Finally we can see the back of my terrace come into view. Normally at this point if I am with someone new, I go into detail about the houses and the square; that they were built in 1840; that each one on the square had a separate coach house. When we bought ours the fireplaces were all blocked up and we found marble masterpieces behind the plasterboard; how the builder took up wretched, patterned, 1960s carpet and found wide, solid, nine inch oak floorboards underneath. I restored all the original cornice work and painted each room in authentic nineteenth-century colours. It is all now so irrelevant.

But today it is different. Today I don't care about bricks and mortar. I am possessed by a different devil; the devil of my past.

I jump out of the car before it properly stops and run up the steps. The door is open and Magda and her son Tommy are in the hall, waiting.

Brief introductions to Frank are made. We all sit down in the front drawing-room. 'OK, Tommy,' I say, 'tell us everything that happened.'

8

The Lift

TOMMY HOLDS HIS TEENAGE lankiness awkwardly. His legs seem too long for the couch. His hair keeps falling in front of his eyes and he brushes it away with hands that are stained with homemade tattoos. He looks exhausted.

'It was like this. Me and Jack were messing round after school … you know we always do that on Wednesdays, it's half day and there was no homework 'cos of the special rugby match.'

'Yes, yes, I know that, Tommy.'

'Well we were coming up to the DART station when two guys on motorbikes stopped ahead of us. One of them was doing something to his engine. Anyway they got chatting, they were real friendly.'

'And you just started talking to strangers?'

'They called Jack by his name.'

'How did they know that?'

'They said they were in school a couple of years ahead of us. That they left last year.'

'Do you remember them from school, Tommy?'

'Well, no, but it's a big school, like they could have been there.'

'I think that's odd,' says Frank. 'When I was in school I knew the boys above me but never below.'

'Yes, same here,' agrees Karl.

'Jack stands out a bit though, he's unusual. So it could have been true,' I add. 'Just carry on, Tommy.'

'They started telling us all about their bikes, they were big bikes, Yamaha 650s, I think, but I'm not sure. After a couple of minutes they asked where we were headed. Jack said Sandycove and they said they were going out as far as Greystones so they might as well give us a ride.'

'What about helmets, Tommy? I've told Jack never to get up on a motorbike, especially without a helmet.'

'They had passenger helmets in the back carrier things; you know, those boxy things on the back of bikes? Said they were for their girlfriends. So, so,' and Tommy's eyes go all watery and his breath is coming in and out in gasps.

'Come on, Tommy, I know this is hard but we have to know everything,' I say as softly as I can manage. 'You're not in trouble, Tommy.'

'We couldn't believe our luck so we hopped on. Except, except – I got nervous immediately because I lost sight of Jack almost at once. His bike seemed to speed off at a really fast pace. My guy took it quite easy by comparison. But the funny thing was when we got to the station at Sandycove he, my biker, just dumped me and drove off and he had been real friendly before. I waited there for half an hour and started getting worried when Jack didn't turn up. I kept hoping that they'd taken a different route. Then I started thinking maybe they'd crashed. I tried his phone but it was switched off. Then I rang Mum and she came and got me.'

'You've told the guards all this?' asks Frank.

'Yes, over and over.'

'You've checked all the hospitals?'

Tommy's tears start at last. Magda, sitting beside him, puts her arm around his shoulder.

'Yes, I did that before I even rang Karl,' says Magda. I notice she has smudged her eyeliner and black streaks are running down her face. Her long curly black hair looks dishevelled. She looks like she hasn't slept all night. Of all the people that would be concerned for Jack I know Magda would have done her very best to find him. Tommy and Jack have known each other since playschool. They are as close as brothers.

'There's nothing, no report of a motorbike accident in any of the Dublin hospitals. I have tried them all.'

'Accents, Tommy, what sort of accents did they have?' I continue, as Tommy seems to have recovered slightly.

'I don't know, they sounded a bit Dub, but at the same time just like me and Jack. But … but one of them did most of the talking, I noticed that. The other guy seemed a bit uncomfortable with the whole thing.'

'Age?' I ask.

'Nineteen or twenty I would say … like they were so friendly, how were we supposed to know?'

'Description?' asks Frank.

'They looked just like regular guys to us, I can't give a good description, the guards already asked.'

Tommy is getting upset again. I can see it coming.

'Look,' says Karl, 'we have been up all night and gone over and over this territory. You aren't going to discover anything new.'

It's at times like these that I really hate Karl. The way he dismisses my opinion negates my very existence. I try not to show it. I swear to myself that I will leave him when this is all over. But when will this be over and when will Jack be found? What can I do to make sense of it all?

'Tommy, you know how you're great at drawing? How about you try and draw what they were like?' I suggest.

'Yeah, I think I could do that.'

'That's a good idea,' says Frank. 'Try and put in everything, the bikes, the colour of their jackets and helmets, anything. Now—'

He is interrupted by the phone ringing in the hallway. We are all momentarily stunned.

'Have the guards put a trace on your line yet?' Frank asks.

'They've done fuck all,' says Karl.

'Is there an extension somewhere, Helen?'

'Yes, upstairs on the landing.'

'OK, you answer it upstairs and I'll pick up down here at the same time, right?'

'Right, OK,' I say as I leg it up the stairs two at a time, hoping to God it doesn't ring off before I reach it.

9

The Truth

'OK, HAVE YOU GOT IT?' Frank shouts.

'Yes … on the count of three,' I call down the stairs.

'One two three … pick up.'

A sickly sweet monotone voice says, 'This is the Eircom answering service. There are two, new messages, in your mailbox.'

'Christ, Frank, it's only the damn messaging service.'

'Listen to them, Helen, listen,' says Frank from the hall below.

'To listen to your voice messages press 1.'

I dutifully press 1.

'First message sent yesterday at ten-thirty-five p.m.'

'Karl, it's me Magda, I have been trying your mobile for hours, I've been round to your house and the gallery but there's no answer. Please call me, Karl. It's really urgent. It's about Jack, he's gone missing. Please call me, Karl, on my mobile.'

'Second message sent yesterday at eleven o-five p.m.'

'Jack it's Dad … your Dad here, Jack,' says a slurred voice. 'I've … I've just been delayed here with a few clients. I'm not sure where you're supposed to be tonight, Jack. Is it Magda's house or ours? I tried your mobile but it's on answering. I'm sure you're OK, you're well able to look after yourself, I know that, maybe you're in with Magda anyway … I'll see you later.'

I put down the phone slowly and go downstairs. I am beginning to simmer with anger.

Karl and Magda have worked out what has gone on. I notice Karl has opened a bottle of red wine and is gulping down a glass. He looks at me with a sense of dread in his eyes. A little boy caught out again by his mother. Magda looks awful.

'So, Karl, perhaps you'd like to tell me what time you got back here last night and what time you reported Jack missing to the police?'

Magda replies before he has a chance.

'I went to the police at six in the evening, Helen, but because I wasn't a parent, or in sole charge of Jack, it wasn't an official report till Karl turned up. I tried your mobile, Helen, loads of times but it must have been out of coverage.'

Ignoring Magda, I repeat the question. 'What time was it reported, Karl?'

He takes another gulp of wine and looks at his feet. Now I am going to explode.

'Karl? Karl,' I say. 'will you tell me the fucking truth, you bastard?'

'OK, OK,' he says, and puts his hands up in defence just in case I do actually hit him. 'I messed up. I met a client after work for a drink. One thing led to another, he insisted on me going to dinner with him in the new Saddle Room, you know how it is, Helen?'

'Yes, I know how it is with you, Karl; now what time did you get back here?'

'About midnight, Magda was waiting.'

'I used your spare key, Helen, the one under the steps,' says Magda unnecessarily.

'Magda forced a pot of coffee down me and we went to the police at one o'clock.'

'No wonder you were there all night,' comments Frank drily.

'Oh my God, I can't believe this, how much worse can things get?' I say.

Magda begins to cry. I am torn between wanting to comfort her and wanting to beat the living daylights out of Karl.

I try to settle down. I am not a violent person, I keep repeating to myself. I just want to blame someone for all of this. Karl is always such an easy target.

Frank takes over.

'Look, we've got a lot of threads here, let's try and make some sense of them before we go off blaming each other. It sounds like a well-planned abduction to me.'

'What do you mean?' I ask.

'How often do you go and visit your mother for instance? Are you frequently away from Jack at night?'

'No, hardly ever; I hate leaving him.'

'So who knew you were going to Cillindara? How did they know where to pick him up after school?'

'My mother is dying, Frank. I had to go and see her. Are you suggesting there is a connection?'

'Yes, of course, I'm suggesting a connection. You only have to look at the note to know that.'

'You mean it was planned so that I would be out of the way.'

'Maybe, Helen, maybe.'

A moment of quiet descends upon us all. Frank is looking confused.

'Who was this client anyway? Do you know him a long time, Karl?' he asks.

Karl has decided to take on an honest tone at last.

'Actually no, it's only the second time I met him.'

'Then there's the guy on the train who gave me the note. Someone must know who he is,' I add.

I notice Karl looking slightly uncomfortable, perhaps he is just as perplexed as the rest of us.

'I think we should ring Charlie,' I suggest.

'What about the business card? Can we check that Hayes guy out?' Frank asks. 'I'm going to make a few calls. I know plenty of people in the legal fraternity in Dublin who at least might know of this solicitor and what kind of law he specializes in.'

'Look, I'm sure the guards will know how to proceed from here,' says Karl.

'The guards? Are you totally mad, Karl? Do you think I am going to get the guards involved when the note specifically says not to?'

Karl takes on an officious stance.

'Helen, we will have to get the guards involved,' he says. 'How would we ever forgive ourselves if something happened to Jack and we hadn't given them the opportunity to help us?'

I want to tell Karl to shut up. I can't think straight. Nothing bad is going to happen to Jack, I keep saying to myself. Nothing bad. Nothing bad. I can't think about that. I'll just end up in a heap on the floor crying if I even start to go there.

'Helen, I need to talk to you in private,' says Karl.

The last thing I feel like doing is talking to Karl alone. I find it hard enough to be in the same room as him. All the work I have done on trying to tolerate him in this marriage just seems to have evaporated into thin air. I just can't help blaming him for everything.

'OK, Karl, but give me a minute, will you? There are too many things spinning around in my head.'

'Helen, it's important.'

'So was telling me the truth about what happened last night, Karl.' Things are beginning to heat up again. Frank intervenes.

'Let's consider our leads so far. I suggest we take a break for twenty minutes or half an hour and reconvene with ideas of where to go next.'

'I'm going to take a shower,' I announce, glaring at Karl.

'Karl, maybe you could do a bit more homework on that client before we cut him out of the loop,' says Frank.

He nods in agreement. I stand, stunned, looking at Frank, the anger draining out of me and being replaced by rational common sense. I can see why he runs such a successful company. I am relieved to have someone take charge. For the first time in years I have a strange longing to be back in boarding-school with the timetable for the term set out and each minute of the day mapped out and ordered. I want to hear the headmistress barking orders. 'I'll do what I'm told this time. I promise.'

I go upstairs, my legs feeling like lead, and drag myself into the shower. I let the hot water sizzle on my skin for longer than I know.

I don't want to leave the warm comfort of the steamy cubicle. I dry myself roughly and wander out to the hot press looking for clean laundry.

The door of Jack's room is open and I go in. His duvet is slung across the bed. Was it only yesterday that I got him up for school? It seems like days ago.

The smell of him is everywhere, from his clothes thrown randomly on the floor to his painstakingly painted figures of warriors in full combat gear. His maths copy peeps out from under the bed, forgotten again. Old worn posters of Gandalf, Legolas and Aragorn adorn the walls. There is a newer one of Harry Potter. His electric guitar is propped up against the bed end, playstation CDs on his desk all seem to be out of their covers. His computer is decorated with chunky graffiti. There's a poster of Kate Moss striking a provocative pose on his wall. His Lynx aftershave is missing its top. The boy is becoming a man.

I lie down on his duvet and make a conscious decision not to break down. I need to get inside myself and work out where to go from here. I allow my eyes to close, just for minute, to concentrate.

Within an instant there are pictures in my mind replaying the events of the last twenty-four hours. I am searching for a missing link. Nothing happens; there is no moment of enlightenment. I allow myself to breathe deeper and force myself to relax in the hope that I will think of something obvious which has eluded me so far. I am fighting the desire to sleep, but at the same time wanting the relief of blankness, an anaesthetic for the pain inside.

As I lay drifting, a new picture of my past comes into my mind. I am back in the time when I lived in the little house at Hill Street in Cillindara village. My mother wasn't home from work yet and I was playing in the back lane with Mary Ellen Reilly. We were joking and laughing and following a frog jump in and out of the puddles. Mary Ellen's da emerged from one of the back garden gates. He had finished his job and it was time for Mary Ellen to go home. He tidied his tools into a thick belt around his waist. He crouched down on his hunkers and bade us to come nearer. He took a ten pence coin out of his pocket and rubbed it in-between his palms. When he opened his hands it had disappeared and then he made it reappear from behind his ear. Mary Ellen and me were all a wonder. I wanted to have a magic dad like him and wished I could be Mary Ellen travelling around from town to town with all my relations.

Just then I heard my mother's voice from the bottom of the lane. She was calling me. I made to scarper but, too late, she found me with the Reillys. The exchange between her and Mr Reilly was brief and curt. As soon as we were out of view, she walloped me behind the ear. It was the first time I ever remember her being angry with me.

'No daughter of mine shall associate with tinkers, do you hear me, girl, do you hear me? Don't let me ever see you talk to the likes of them again.' The violence of the scene jolts me awake. I must have only drifted off for two or three minutes. I am still smarting when I hear a polite knock on the door. It's Magda.

'Come on, Helen, you are needed downstairs.'

10

The Lies

MAGDA IS LOOKING A little better now than when we came in. Her make-up has been reapplied and most of her usual air of calmness has returned. As she walks into the room I can hear her bracelets jangle and smell the familiar scent of her jasmine perfume.

'Magda, look, Magda, I'm not angry with you, you know that don't you? It's Karl, he's always so blasé about the way he minds Jack and now look what's happened.'

'Sure, Helen, I know that; we will have plenty of time to go over everything later.'

Magda gives me a big hug and I know I am going to start crying. I pull away from her. I want to keep logical and rational. I can't afford to let my emotions come in and break me down.

'Who is that man Frank anyway? He really seems to be taking charge down there,' she asks.

'Oh, he's a friend of Charlie's, you know the older man who works for my mother? He's been with her for years.'

'Yes, I have heard you talk about Charlie but never about Frank. Are you sure about him? Why is he getting involved?'

'He seems to think he owes the family a favour in some way. He happens to own a large building company and has offered us cash if we need it to get Jack back. Why? Don't you trust him?'

'I don't know. To be honest I am so shocked that I just don't know who to trust, Helen.'

'I know what you mean. It's just that I used to know him, down on the estate when I was younger. I like him. He seems to know what he's doing. I find something reassuring about him and you know how bad it is with me and Karl. He can act as a buffer.'

I sense that she is disappointed that I have not immediately included her.

'You'd be too likely to take my side in everything, Magda.'

She smiles and I know that she agrees with me.

'I suppose that's a good point. It's just the atmosphere downstairs between him and Karl is very edgy. I mean Karl is obviously upset about Jack but ... but ...'

'What, Magda? What else could there possibly be that would be worse than Jack being missing?'

'Apart from the fact that they blatantly don't like each other? I can sense that, but Karl is very nervous. He's drinking wine, for God's sake, and he's hardly sobered up from last night. He just got a call from the gallery and went white as a sheet.'

'Let me get some clothes on and see what is going on.'

I throw on a pair of jeans and a T-shirt. I know that Magda wouldn't have said anything to me unless she had genuinely worked out something was up. She knows me and Karl backwards. I should have listened to whatever it was Karl wanted to say to me earlier, but my communication with him has been so fractured of late that I generally find it easier to avoid it altogether.

I race downstairs, annoyed with myself for drifting off in Jack's room. I have been wasting time.

I find Karl and Frank huddled in conversation. I hear the name Katherine mentioned. That's my mother's name, so I presume they are talking about her illness.

'Helen,' says Karl, who does indeed look to be paler than usual. 'The guards are on their way. We are going to get to the bottom of this, don't worry.'

'Don't worry', that's the understatement of the year I feel like saying, but I don't want this to turn into the regular bitching sessions I have with him.

'Look, I already told you, I don't think we should let the guards in on this. Not yet anyway.'

'Yes, I'm worried about that, too,' Frank agrees. 'Come to think of it what have they got to go on at this stage? There's a boy who doesn't know the model of the motorbikes. There are no number plates, no positive IDs, no demand for money, and no location.'

'That's exactly why we should hand it over to the guards,' snaps Karl, 'it's too big for us to handle on our own.'

'I agree with Frank,' I say. 'I have a feeling we're being watched or something. If we involve the guards I think they, the kidnappers, will know.'

Karl is raging with anger. Frank is staring him down. They are glaring at each other with mutual and intense dislike. Whatever has gone on while I was upstairs, Magda's summation of the vibe between them is correct. They can't stand each other. I look at them both – Karl, the man I live with and the father of my son, and Frank, the man I have just met. Why am I more inclined to side with Frank? What makes his judgement better than Karl's? I instinctively trust him and am drawn to him in some sort of strange way that I can't explain. None of this is making sense.

The phone rings again. We look at each other fearfully. Frank motions me to answer.

'Hello.'

'Is that Helen Rafferty?' says a voice that is immediately recognizable as the man from the train.

'Yes, yes, it's me.'

'Call the guards off now, do you understand? Call them off, or you won't see Jack again.'

'But, but let me talk to Jack, let—'

The phone clicks and the call is ended.

Shaking, I go back into the drawing-room. Clearly something is wrong.

'What is it, Helen, who was it?'

'It's him, it's the man on the train; he knows the guards are coming. We have to call them off. I told you, Karl, I told you.'

'Are you sure, Helen? Are you sure it was him?'

'Yes, yes, of course I am. We have to call them off.'

The bell in the hall sounds and we know that it will be the Gardaí. We hurriedly agree that we will try and play down the whole incident last night. We haven't time to work out the exact details of how we are going to do this. Magda lets in two plain clothes policemen. They are dressed in dark suits. They look younger than I had expected. Both of them are clean shaven with short hair. One wears glasses and is taller than Karl. That makes him over six feet anyway. He has short black hair, balding at the temples. His colleague is smaller and fairer and wears a tie that clashes with his shirt. He looks slightly younger. They are both serious and professional in their demeanour. They immediately make their way over to me. I am completely flustered.

They flash their IDs but in my panic I can hardly see them, let alone read them.

'Are you Helen Rafferty?' asks the older of the two.

I am surprised at the gentleness of his tone. I had expected it to be more accusatory. I have an easy ability to feel always at fault.

'Yes, I am.'

'Are you the mother of Jack Rafferty?'

'Yes, yes, I am.'

'I'm Detective Eammon Malone and this is my colleague, Jimmy O'Meara. We are here to ask you a few questions about the disappearance of your son Jack.'

'Jack, that's right, Jack.'

'We need you to confirm that your son is missing?'

I have no idea what to do. How do I answer him? What excuse am I going to make?

'Mrs Rafferty, the disappearance of your son. He is missing I take it?'

'Jack, Jack,' is all I can manage to say.

Frank at least has the presence of mind to intervene.

'Detective Malone, there has been a lot of confusion here. We've all been in a terrible panic but the thing is Jack is not missing at all.'

'Oh, he's not missing?' Detective Malone raises his eyebrows and turns to his colleague. There is a slight change now in his tone. 'Take notes, O'Meara, we may need this later on.'

O'Meara takes out a little black notebook and starts writing.

'No, no, he's not missing. He's down in Helen's family house in Cillindara. Isn't that right, Helen?'

'Yes,' I say suddenly realizing what Frank is up to. 'He's in my mother's house. I brought him down there yesterday after school. I'm sorry for all the confusion. Karl, erm, Karl never got a message about it that's all.'

The detectives aren't looking too happy about this explanation. I am looking at Karl and Magda hoping that one of them will back me up.

'Mrs Rafferty we were led to believe your son was abducted on a motorbike after school. Are you now saying that his friend Tommy Lavery, who I see over there with his mother, was making this all up?'

'No, no, not at all, Detective, it's just that I was waiting at the DART station in Sandycove for Jack. And, erm, I went straight from there. I had every intention of ringing Karl and Magda on the way down but my phone was out of battery. I left a message for Karl as soon as I arrived but he never picked it up.'

Detective Malone turns to Magda.

'Can you confirm this story, Ms Lavery?'

'If Helen says Jack is in her mother's house, of course I believe her, Detective, is that what you are asking? The whole thing was terribly unfortunate. Karl, I mean Mr Rafferty, was out with a client. We explained this last night to you Detective. Unfortunately we all got our wires crossed. I'm so sorry I made such a fuss.'

'I have to take responsibility for it too, Detective Malone,' says Karl. 'If I hadn't got delayed with this client and if I had bothered to check my messages none of this would have occurred.'

'Tell me, Mr Rafferty, was it a voice message or a text message that your wife left on your phone?'

Karl is stopped in his tracks for a couple of seconds. Go on Karl, go on, I am willing him. Act quickly, don't blow it, we are nearly there.

'A voice message, Detective.'

'Well, in that case, do you mind if I listen to it now, Mr Rafferty?'

Karl shrugs his shoulders and raises his hands.

'Sorry, Detective, no can do, I get so many calls that I have got into the habit of deleting them as I hear them.'

I notice the detective getting a little flushed. Our explanation does not exactly stand up with him. O'Meara begins to walk around the drawing-room, observing, taking everything in. He strolls over to the mantelpiece and stares at the print above it. It is of no significance, a 1930s' pen and ink drawing that I salvaged from a run down house that I renovated. It is odd that he appears so interested in it. I feel invaded.

'I ... I am not too happy with this at all. We have received an official complaint that your son is missing and until we have proof that this is not the case I am legally bound to investigate this matter. I think we are going to have to interview you all separately down at the station to get to the bottom of this, Mrs Rafferty. And, by the way, we haven't been introduced to this man here,' he says, swivelling around on his heels and pointing to Frank.

'I'm Frank Callan; my apologies, a family friend from Cillindara, Detective Malone,' says Frank. 'Do you think I could have a word with you both in private, Detectives?' he asks.

'I don't see where that's going to get you, Mr Callan.'

'There are some family considerations I think you should take into account.'

I haven't a clue what Frank is on about, but if it gets Malone and O'Meara off the trail I will go along with it. Perhaps he is going to use the fact that my mother is dying as some sort of excuse.

'If you insist,' says Malone.

'Helen, would you mind if we went into the kitchen? Maybe you could see if young Tommy there is all right?'

He gives me a quick wink and I realize that Tommy is sitting by the drawing of the boys who took Jack.

'Right, of course, Frank, go ahead.'

I make my way over to Tommy and quietly take the picture he has almost finished before Detective O'Meara notices. I place it between the newspapers on the sideboard. I think I can see Frank give me another wink. I hope I am doing the right thing. The sound of the kidnapper's voice on the phone is still in my head.

Karl is looking hassled. He takes another call on his mobile. I can tell from the tone of his voice that something else truly bad has happened.

'What's the matter, Karl?' I ask, when the detectives and Frank have gone into the kitchen.

'The gallery has been raided by the fraud squad. They have been crawling all over the place for hours. They have found some, some …'

'Some what? Karl, what?'

'Some stolen paintings, Helen. I think I'm going to be arrested.'

11

The Party

AFTER SEVERAL MINUTES FRANK and the detectives come out of the kitchen. Whatever Frank has said to them they appear a lot more relaxed. Malone has agreed to defer further investigations on condition that we produce Jack at the police station here or at Cillindara within the next twenty-four hours.

'I am not at all sure what is going on here, Mrs Rafferty, but I understand that your mother is seriously ill and I do understand that people can get mixed up when they are under emotional pressure. You should have told us about your family situation. However, it does not change the fact that we will have to be satisfied of your son's safety before we close off on the complaint. Mr Callan informs me that you are going back to Cillindara today so I suggest you take Jack to the Garda station there. Once the sergeant there has seen Jack and can attest to his safety we can let the matter lie. Is that all right with you?'

'Yes, of course, I am so sorry for wasting your time like this, Detective Malone.'

His tone appears soft and empathetic but I am still not sure that we have entirely convinced him. He surveys the room slowly looking at each one of us for confirmation. I suspect he does not believe us, but I think we might have just got away with this.

'Oh, we will need a recent photograph of Jack so that we can fax it down to the station and the sergeant can match descriptions when you produce him,' he says.

'Yes, of course,' I say and move towards a drawer in the sideboard to take out a photo. Its painful looking through the last lot of photos I had developed, but I manage to get a recent one without breaking down. Frank is nearest to me and I hand it to him to give to the detective. He takes the photo and examines it carefully.

I notice the expression change on Frank's face when he looks at the image. He's shocked but trying desperately to hide it.

'He's a good-looking boy all right,' he says, with an almost forced casualness after a moment or two and then gives the photograph to Detective Malone.

The detectives move towards the hallway and I see them out. As soon as they are out of earshot I ask Frank, 'You had an odd reaction to the photo. Have you seen Jack before?'

He brushes me off. 'Me? No, no way, Helen. How could I have?'

But there is some change in his tone that does not allay my suspicions.

'He reminds me of someone that's all.'

For the first time I begin to doubt him. I think he is lying.

'I can't believe we got away with that.'

'We have just bought some time that's all.'

'Let's hope it was the right thing to do,' says Karl.

After a few minutes we begin to reassemble our thoughts when the doorbell rings again. I open it and am faced with two further suited gentlemen. This time I see a squad car parked opposite the house.

'We are looking for Karl Rafferty,' says one of them.

Karl comes forward and identifies himself.

'Mr Rafferty, do you own the Grayman Gallery at 1566 Molesworth Street, Dublin 2?'

'Yes, I do.'

'Then it is my duty to inform you that further to our investigations on your premises we believe you may be complicit in the supply and sale of stolen goods. You are requested to accompany us to the station forthwith and assist us with our enquiries.'

Karl looks like he is going to faint.

'I don't know what you are talking about. This is entirely ridiculous. There must be a grievous error on your part. I run a legitimate business. This is preposterous,' Karl says, but his tone is guilty.

'If you have no idea what we are talking about, Mr Rafferty, perhaps you would like to explain that in a statement at the station.'

'Karl, go with the detectives, will you, and clear this up. We need to be getting on with things here, if you get my meaning.'

'All right, Helen, I'll go with them, but I refuse to make a statement until I see my solicitor. Phone my solicitor immediately, will you, and tell him what's happened? And come down to the station; I have to talk to you, Helen.'

I open the door for them and check that Malone and O'Meara have definitely gone and am relieved to realize the two lots of detectives did not cross paths. I think Malone's attitude would have been entirely different if he had just witnessed this. I wonder how long it will take him to find out. Karl is led down the front steps by these two new policemen.

It all happens so quickly I am completely stunned. I am trying to get things in perspective here. My son, my boy Jack is missing. My precious boy. How dare anyone take him? What do they want? I have a ransom note that doesn't make sense so I don't know how to get him back. I can't get the guards involved for fear of them hurting him. Now Karl has just been arrested, again.

I close the door behind them and walk in silence to the kitchen. There is some cold coffee in the cafetiére which I pour out into a sugared mug. Frank tries to speak to me but I bid him silence.

Karl arrested; arrested again, is all I can think about.

I sit down and take a gulp and try and think about where to go from here.

I can't get rid of the image of Karl being led down the steps. It brings me back. I try not to let it but it happens anyway.

I am back at the party all those years ago at Karl's place in Morehampton Road. Crowds of people were scattered about. A lot of them I didn't know although they knew me. They knew me because I was with Karl, no other reason. I'm his latest 'bit of skirt'

I hear one of them say. 'Like your new wallpaper', says another. Karl was a lot older than me and so were his friends. Sometimes they made me feel nervous with their patronizing remarks and coded put-downs. I didn't understand them. But I didn't care about them. All I cared about was Karl. I see him now as he was then; his long blond hair tied back in a ponytail, his signature cowboy boots and jeans. I remember driving around with him in his red sports car against the grey Dublin sky. I looked up to Karl then. He talked. I listened. I believed. Back then he was *the man* to be around. Of course, there was bit of dealing on the side, which was part of his attraction. He always had a constant supply of illegal substances, a bit of dope here, a line of coke there, heads from Thailand, speed from Amsterdam. He supplied to all the *right* people.

I remember how he scored that night; a film canister of pure white powder all the way from Santa Cruz, the heart of the cocaine trade in Bolivia. 'It came first class, darling', he tells me which meant it came directly on a flight with a friend of his; untouched and uncut. I hoovered up a couple of lines in the bedroom just to put me in the mood. I floated about downstairs in a long summer evening dress, trying to talk to people but not being terribly successful at it. The pubs closed and the crowd in the flat began to swell. I don't think Karl had a clue who half these people were. I smoked a few joints and ended up dancing with some strangers. Someone handed me a bottle of blue Smirnoff. I drank several large swigs straight by the neck. The room started to spin. I thought I was going to get sick. Karl saw me and got cross. He directed me upstairs 'for a little rest, Helen'.

I lay down, fully clothed, and sank into a deep substance-induced sleep. Total blankness for a little while. Then I started dreaming that Karl had come into the room. I could still hear the thumping of the music downstairs so the line between sleep and reality was thin. He asked me if I was feeling better and I asked him to come over. I wanted him to hold me, to tell me that everything would be all right. He hugged me softly for a while and then made to go again but I pleaded with him to stay. After a few minutes we began to make love, really make love, not like the functional sex that we normally had, this time he was gentle and caring and loving like he had never been before. The touch was different. He kept calling my name, 'Helen, Helen, I always wanted you', but in my inebriated state the voice was distant. When it was over I was strangely happy, like I had never been before. I didn't know that this was how love should be. Later, I woke and saw Karl's body sprawled on the bed beside me. I drifted off into a deep and happy sleep trying to recreate our love-making in my head.

Next thing I knew it's very early in the morning. I was lying naked in Karl's bed and he woke up suddenly. The banging on the door was ridiculously loud. 'Police, police, open up', is all I could hear.

Karl scrambled out of bed and tried to gather up his drugs. The banging wouldn't stop.

'Quick, Helen, get up, will you? Find the drugs, any drugs, and get them out of here,' he was shouting.

But I was feeling half dead, my reactions were too slow. I remembered coming to bed, but I couldn't remember taking my clothes off. Snatches of my sexual encounter came back to me but I dismissed them as a dream and, like all dreams, I soon forgot the details.

Normally as I wake I would have a few minutes to piece the night before together. But then the banging stopped suddenly and there was silence. Then there was an awful cracking sound and I realized the police had broken the flat door down. I hadn't even got my underwear on. I was standing in the bedroom naked when four or five policemen burst in. The humiliation of it all comes back. Some of them were smirking at me. Karl didn't even try to shield me. He did nothing to protect me. A senior officer handed me a sheet to cover myself with. 'You're so young', he said in disgust, 'you should go home to your mother, a nice girl like you'. I was far from nice I felt. Far from that.

Karl said afterwards that that guard made it really hard for him at the station. After a short search of the flat, where there was ample evidence of illegal substances, Karl was arrested and taken away in handcuffs. I was given a few minutes to dress and hauled down to the police station in a different car. They had nothing on me. It wasn't my flat and possession charges would never stand up in court. After a grilling, where I claimed complete ignorance, I was let go. But Karl was charged; that was really the beginning of the end.

Fifteen years later and the whole thing is happening again. It's happening just when I don't need it too. Just like before. Why has he always abandoned me?

Frank and Magda are in the kitchen looking at each other and then looking on me with pity. Quite suddenly I am angry. I don't want their pity; I want my son back. I can't waste time trying to get Karl off the hook. I'll ring the solicitor later and let him sort it out. I am certainly not going down to the station to talk to him.

'OK, Frank, Magda, let's get organized and work out exactly what we are going to do from here.'

12

The Facts

WE GO UPSTAIRS INTO my office. I clean the whiteboard and take a marker in my hand. I write out the first line of the ransom note. *Find your father's will.*

The three of us agree that there are two possibilities here: my real father, or Edgar Royston, my stepfather.

'In light of the fact that your mother is dying, don't you think it's referring to Edgar?' asks Frank.

I consider this for a few moments but dismiss it.

'I just don't see how that could be. There has to be a motive for the kidnapping and as far as I can see they, the kidnappers, must be after money. Edgar's will, whatever is in it, is irrelevant to me as I am not due to inherit anything from the estate. It's to be distributed between his blood relatives only, nephews and nieces and the like, of which there are plenty. My mother only has a life tenancy to the house and a caretaking agreement to the estate. The ownership of the house and land reverts to the nearest Royston bloodline in the event of her death.'

Frank shakes his head in disbelief.

'But surely he would have left you something, Helen? You were his stepdaughter after all and you have often talked about how fond of you he was,' says Magda.

'Yes, that is true, but my mother consistently told me, in many of her rages, that I deserved nothing and that she would make sure that I got nothing.'

I see Frank looking perplexed. Magda has some understanding of what I am talking about, but I certainly don't want to start explaining my acrimonious relationship with my mother to him, so I continue.

'We only have a couple of hours before Detective Malone will be on to us. I think it is much more likely that the ransom note is referring to my real father's will. I have been thinking over it all day long. Thinking why on earth my mother was so secretive about him? Sure, I made excuses for her when I was growing up. I used to think it would upset her to show me my father's grave. Then I thought that maybe Edgar was sensitive about my real father and didn't want any mention of him in our lives. But now, now I am beginning to suspect that he's been alive all this time, or even recently deceased. Perhaps he knew about me and that's why he disappeared in the States all those years ago. If I can prove I am his daughter maybe his will is compromised in some way. That's all I can think of.'

Frank starts to disagree with me, but I ask him to wait until I have finished.

I write out the second sentence of the ransom note on the board: *a house you lived in when you were young.*

'I only know of living in Hill Street and occasionally Cillindara. But, as you correctly pointed out on the train, Frank, I must have lived somewhere else before that, before I was four. I am sure that my mother never owned the house in Hill Street so perhaps it was rented on when we left or sold. Either way it is most likely occupied by someone else now so we would have difficulty accessing it. I can check this later, but I don't think the ransom note is directing us there. I think we need to start at where I was born, assuming that wherever that is, it's going to be closer to the mystery of my real father. I can see, Frank, that you are not entirely convinced of my strategy. Neither am I, but I have to make a decision and go with it. We only have two options and very little time, so we have to do something.'

'Not at all, Helen. I think you could well be on to something here, but what I don't know is, how we are going to find out.'

'I've thought of that. The primary source of information in all of this is plainly my mother but, going by the state she was in yesterday, I am never going to get any sense out of her. The only other source is Charlie; he was "from home" my mother always said, so I am going to start there. I'll ring him and in the meantime you could check out this solicitor and find out about this town land.'

'No problem, I'm already on to it,' he says and he disappears down the stairs. I turn to Magda; she looks at me curiously.

'What is it? What's the matter?'

'Nothing, nothing at all, Helen. I have just never seen you in work mode like this before. I'm just so used to you being Jack's mother and—'

'Karl's compliant wife?'

'Yes.'

'Magda, I think it's time the real Helen Rafferty took over, don't you?'

'Yes,' she smiles. 'What do you want me to do?'

'The client, the one Karl went out with last night. Can you ring Evelyn, Karl's assistant in the gallery and get her to give you any information about him? And the drawing of Tommy's, I put it between some papers on the sideboard. Can you get it and I will have a look at it after I talk to Charlie?'

Magda agrees to my requests and leaves the office. I am left alone to make the call.

Again Charlie answers quickly and again, it's hard to get him to talk about my father. I have to tease the information out of him. He was always such a reserved man, Charlie, and now I am questioning probing, grilling him for every smidgen of information that he might hold about my mother and father and their past. It doesn't sit well with him, but eventually, with coaxing, he starts to open up.

'Tell me where I lived when I was small, Charlie. Did I live in Donntra or was it Cork with my mother?'

'Oh no, you lived with your mother and grandmother in your

own home place. Your mother had left those legal people from Montenotte before you were born.'

'Can you remember their names, Charlie? The solicitors' names?'

'Oh, you have me there now, girl. I couldn't tell you.'

'Why did she move back to Donntra then? Was it something to do with having me? Why didn't she stay on with them?'

'No, no, this was all before you were born. Your grandfather had died several years previous and your grandmother was on her own. She got poorly and Katherine was obliged to come back and look after her. It was a big disappointment for her, of course, leaving all that high society behind. But she got on with it; your mother was never one for moaning.'

'Wasn't she?' I say in way of disbelief, but Charlie doesn't notice.

'Mind you, it wasn't all that bad for her; she got a job in Donntra, at Green's. They were a big Protestant firm, agricultural suppliers, seeds and fertilizer and big farm machinery. Every farmer in the county came into Green's at some stage of the year. She was well liked and well sought after. That was before, you know, before you came along like.'

Charlie goes on to tell me that my mother led an isolated existence in the country, living with her mother, after I was born. She wasn't allowed to keep on her job at Green's Seeds and Supplies in the town and, as far as he could work out, she was shunned by Daniel's family and the locals for having a child out of wedlock.

'Tell me where I lived with her then. Was it in the town itself, or outside? That's all I need to know.'

'Sure, don't you know yourself you are from farming stock? We, that is Daniel, your mother and I all came from small farms in the same town land.'

'What was that called, Charlie?'

'Ballytain. Didn't she ever bring you back to your own home place?'

Oh my God, it's the name on the back of the business card. Everything is connecting me to this place. It is as if I was meant to be directed there. Is this where they have Jack? Is the will hidden there?

'No, I never went there, I'm sure of it. Did she ever go back?'

'I don't know, Helen, I can't answer you that. Your mother was always going away, a couple of days here and there, buying antiques and art pieces for the house. I never asked.'

I get a general description of my mother's house from him as I feel sure I will be going there.

'And you didn't talk about home with her?'

'Rarely, Helen, rarely. We only once spoke of Daniel. And that was when she told me that I needn't mention him in front of Mr Royston. She didn't want any talk of him at all. Well, I could understand that and all, the position she was in, and I respected her in that. So that left Ballytain out of it really. I couldn't separate that place from him.'

He asks me again about the guards.

'So you have to produce Jack at the station? This is madness, girl, madness.' I notice he raises his voice as he says this. Does he want someone else in the room to hear, or is he just a bit anxious?

I decide not to tell him about Karl. It would be too much for him and serve no purpose.

He urges me again to come down to Cillindara to see her, to be with her before she dies. But how can I? How can she put me in this position? That she would choose to die at a time when my son is missing doesn't surprise me. Is it her final act of complete self-interest after she rejected me most of her life? As soon as she met Edgar it seemed like she had no more time for me. That much had always been clear to me. Not that we had had a particularly loving and harmonious relationship before that. We were comfortable with each other though and I adored her, but I always felt she held back. She wasn't physical with me. No hugs or kisses, no sitting on her knee while she told me bedtime stories, only a tiny peck on the cheek before bedtime, pretence at affection. The older I got the less she appeared to love me. I could never understand why she had excluded me from her affections. By the time she married Edgar she could hardly be civil to me. God, how she hated me and is this why? Because she was single and alone in a country village; working in a shop on the accounts; being abandoned by a lover; having me out of wedlock; spoiling her chances for a marriage in Cork. Was that it? Is this why someone took Jack? Is it something to do with my illegitimacy? This is all too much to take in. My brain is in overload. I am swimming in a sea of emotional confusion.

Magda comes back into the office with a disappointed look on her face. She has no useful information about Karl's client.

'Evelyn, the girl in the gallery, couldn't give me a name or contact number for that client. She said Karl is like that; he just goes off on his own and doesn't tell her anything.'

'Yes, I can believe that all right. There's nothing we can do about it, I suppose.'

'She said that as far as she remembered he was a man in his late forties, smartly dressed, that's all.'

'It could be the man on the train, but how can I check that out if she doesn't even know his name?'

'But, there's worse than that, I can't find the drawing Tommy did. I am beginning to think that detective; you know, the younger one, saw you put it there and took it. He was watching you at the time.'

'Damn it. Yes, I felt that too.'

Frank comes back into the office and relays his information about Hayes Cunningham.

'He's a conveyance solicitor, Helen, which means, of course, that he is involved in buying and selling property. I couldn't get to speak to him as he is out of the office and doesn't take calls on his mobile which I find is a ridiculous way to behave these days, but it's a typical mark of his profession. As it happens a colleague of mine knows one of the girls in his office. I got to speak to her and she filled me in on him. He seems like a fairly conservative type, comes from old money. He's very successful. He handles a portfolio of very wealthy clients.'

'Yes, but how is this information going to help us?'

'Ah, let me get to the point. I found out where he is today. He's down in Ballytain, Co. Kerry where a house is being sold at auction. It's only a small little place so my contact thought that it was unusual for him to go all that way for a small property. The auction is on this afternoon. He's acting for the vendor.'

'Well, that's far too much of a coincidence. Ballytain is the town land my father and mother were from and it was written on the back of the card. I have a feeling we are almost being led to this place but I don't know if it is by chance or design. We will have to go down there.'

'But, Helen,' says Magda, 'Kerry is at least six hours away.'

'No, no, it's not,' says Frank. 'Not if you fly.'

13

The Plane

Frank explains that he owns a small plane; a single engine Cessna 150.

'It's in a hangar at Powerscourt Airfield, that's only a fifteen-minute drive from here,' he says.

He goes towards the front window.

'I can see an Opel Vectra parked on the square. It looks like an unmarked Garda car. What's out the back of these houses? Can we get out that way in case this guy is a guard with instructions to follow us?'

'We can go out through the coach house; it leads into a laneway.'

I give Magda our solicitor's number and ask her to call it on behalf of Karl. That's as much I want to do for him. At least I can say I attempted to get him bail. I doubt the solicitor will be able to do much to obtain his release and I suspect he will be arrested. I always knew there was something underhand about Karl's business, but had refused to tackle him head on about it. He can sort his own mess out now. I have to find Jack.

Nobody can find Tommy's drawing. It has completely disappeared without trace. It could have given us some clue as to what Jack's kidnappers looked like. I am beginning to feel hysteria take hold of me.

'Helen, it most likely wouldn't have helped us anyway,' says Frank, but that doesn't reassure me or stop the nauseous feeling rising in my stomach. I quickly run upstairs and throw a few things into a bag. Magda is following me, trying to help, but I know she is about to start crying again. I don't want her to cry. I want her to be brave for me so that I will not crumble, that my world will not fall apart. I think she must sense what I need and she grips my arm tightly. She looks at me resolutely.

'You get going now. Go and get our Jack, go on now.'

Frank has called a taxi and it is to wait at the far end of the back lane. We leave by the back door of the house, go through the garden and reach the archway of the derelict coach house. We emerge into the quiet little lane and begin to make our way to where the taxi should be. I try not to think of all the times I played here with Jack when he was little; running in and out of the neighbours' gardens, hiding in the coach-house doorways. We used to have running races along the mud track but Jack would never wait for the count. He would bolt off before I ever reached the count of three. It became a standing joke with us.

I remember when Jack was five and he picked me a bunch of buttercups from here. It was the first real bunch of flowers he gave me and ever since then buttercups have been my favourite. Now, again, they are in bloom and the sight of them stings me till I am hurting. I am filled with fear.

I see an unfamiliar man in a garden. That's not unusual. I know all the residents who live on the square but some of them have gardeners whom I would not know by sight. It's enough to set the panic in though, and I start running down the lane. That was always my way; to keep running. Frank can't keep up. I have forgotten about his limp. I look back for him and see the man come out of the garden. He has his hand up to his mouth. I imagine he has a hand-held radio in it and is now going to alert the Garda on the square. I see the taxi pull up and jump in. I have to wait about sixty seconds for Frank to catch up. It's a long sixty seconds.

'Jesus, Helen, will you slow down? You'll give me a heart attack. You should have run for Ireland in the last Olympics,' he says as he finally makes it.

The taxi takes off immediately he gets in. The driver seems to

know Frank and where we are going without being told. I look
around but can see no sign of the man from the lane or Gardaí in
an Opel Vectra. I think we have got away. The pace of my breathing
slows.

The drive to Powerscourt is quick and silent. The day is warm
and sunny. If Jack was off school now I would be bringing him,
Tommy and Magda all the way down to Mullagbeg beach in
Wicklow. We'd have the body boards in the back and an ice box full
of fizzy drinks and junk food. I would give out to him for drinking
too much Coke. Magda would have brought a salad with whole-
meal bread and give us a gentle lecture about how we should all
change our diets. When we arrived at the car-park for the public
beach, further up the coast than where we wanted to go, we would
begin our trek across the fields. Through barbed-wire fences,
across a well-worn cattle trail, ignoring the warning signs for stray
bulls on the land, avoiding the stinging nettles, till we reached the
forbidden private dunes. Once there we would set up camp and
spend the afternoon in the soft surf where the waves break and the
water bubbles. Swimming in the water in Mullagbeg is like bathing
in champagne. After we had dried off we would light a fire and cook
some sausages. Magda's would be vegetarian. Jack and Tommy
would climb the giant sand dunes and roll all the way back down,
laughing. When the evening came the boys would plead to stay and
camp down for the night so that they could look up at the stars and
sleep beside the fire. Magda and I, sandy and in need of home
comforts, would say 'next time, boys, next time' and we would all
trek homeward tired and happy. I'm sorry now I didn't let him
camp down there. I'm sorry, Jack.

As we turn off the motorway into the minor roads we are
surrounded by lush, green trees. The ditches are full of wild, white
garlic. I love the smell of it. I open the window to let it in. Frank is
looking at me with concern.

'Are you all right, Helen?'

'Yes, I'm fine,' I lie.

He very softly puts his hand on my shoulder. I notice the difference between him and Karl. Karl was always thin and wiry. There was a bony feel to his hugs. Frank is way bigger, built like a rugby player. There is more of him. He makes me feel safe. He makes me feel minded.

When we get to the airstrip the plane is all fuelled up and ready to go. It looks small. Smaller than anything I have ever flown in before. There are only four seats so I sit up at the cockpit with Frank.

'Are you a nervous flyer?'

'No, I'll be fine.'

He taxis along the runway and takes off smoothly. I never even ask him how long he's been flying planes. I feel I don't need to.

A Cessna doesn't fly as high as a jet plane. It doesn't alienate you from the land and leave you in an anonymous sky. It cruises at about 9,000 ft. I can read it from the altimeter. You feel as if you are still part of the countryside, a distant observer, but still connected to the soil.

The square green fields of Powerscourt change into Coillte pine forests as we go south. We fly over the bog at Kippure and then onto the stilted forest of Kings river. Then, there are great expanses of yellow wheat and large meadows. I see a river.

'That would be the Barrow,' says Frank when I ask.

The settlements along the river look like toy towns from the sky. The stone bridges, the old churches, the narrow streets. Jack would love this. Where are you, Jack? Who has you? What are they doing to you now?

I force myself to keep looking at the ground we are covering. We pass the hill of Cashel and begin to climb into the Galtee mountains.

The constant sound of the engine is making me sleepy. I look at Frank and for the first time I begin to truly remember him. I close my eyes and allow myself to drift back to that summer when I had retreated to the summer-house. I hadn't thought about it for years, not until I met Frank on the train this morning. Was it only this morning? I become aware of how tired I am. My thoughts go back to the parties at the summer-house again. There was a gang of about twenty of us who used to gather there. I had met some girls, with whom I had gone to primary school in the village, and that's how it had all started. They had introduced me to all the lads. I remember Frank all right; he used to hang around with another guy, Neil or Nick, I think his name was. Nick, yes, I'm sure it was Nick. He had black hair and Frank's was redder then. They were both tall, over six foot anyway and when the two of them were together, which was often, they made a striking image. I can see them ambling up the pathway and opening the summer-house door. You always knew the party had begun when those guys arrived.

'Who fancies a number then?' was the usual opening line and the grass would be produced and smoked and before you knew it the music would be louder and the chat would flow freely and the whole place would be buzzing.

They always had girlfriends with them. Frank and Nick had an ability to produce a different blonde each time I met them. They were the type of girls who said very little and just hung out of the boys' arms and looked adoringly into their eyes, as Frank and Nick talked about some money-making scam. It's odd that I have put this all out of my mind until now.

I remember liking Frank even then, but I was so messed up that there was no way anything was going to happen. I think the fact that he had red hair, like me, immediately helped me to relate to him. I used to catch him looking at me when he thought I wasn't looking at him. Was it mutual then?

My mother had never liked my hair and said I looked common with it. She would encourage me to dye it brown. It was just another stick to beat me with. She used to say I looked too Irish. I suspect she was trying to shun her background; that she was ashamed of where she came from. I wish she hadn't taken it out on me.

I'm angry now and fully alert. I sit up and check my watch. I am surprised that I was in that half dreaming state for only ten minutes.

'Do you remember that guy you used to hang around with, Nick somebody or other? Whatever happened to him?' I ask Frank.

'Oh, Nick Grainger, you mean? Yeah he's around; I've done a bit of business with him here and there. Why do you ask?'

Frank takes on a slightly disconcerted stance. Probably the concentration needed to fly.

'No reason; he just came into my head that's all. I thought you two would have been close.'

'We were, we were like that for a long time,' he says and he crosses his index and middle fingers together.

'What happened?'

'A lot. You've seen my limp?'

'Yes, I noticed.'

'I got that on one of the first jobs I did in Dublin with him. A wall fell on top of me, crushing my leg, because Nick had cut corners on the foundation specs. On top of that he hadn't adequately insured the site. After that I decided I couldn't work with him.'

'So you fell out with him over that?'

'No, not immediately; he tried to make it up to me and I stayed friendly with him on a social basis, but in the end I found it hard to be close to someone who'd been married three times. I got sick of breaking it off with his wives. They were nice girls, all of them, but Jesus could that boy fuck them over. I couldn't even begin to tell you. He's with a young one now who's only fit to be his daughter.'

'God, I hate it when guys do that,' I agree.

'Do you?' says Frank, and I redden as I think of the age gap between me and Karl and how it must appear when we are together. I walked straight into that one.

'You were never married, yourself?' I ask.

'Me? No. I had a couple of long-term relationships but none of them worked out. Never met the right woman I suppose.' He looks directly at me when he says this. There's a silence that I don't know how to fill.

The weather changes and we become submerged in cloud. Frank

is on the radio with a calm and confident tone. I am not in any way concerned about the safety of the flight. I feel Frank is in control. He knows what he is doing. There is a break in the cloud and I can see Carrauntoohill in the distance. Then the airstrip at Faranfore comes into view. Frank overshoots it, circles to the right, comes at it again and into a smooth landing.

'Well, that was easy, wasn't it?' I smile.

'Sure, once you get the feel for it, it's hard to give up.'

We get out and go to the nearest car hire desk. An SUV, Frank insists, in case we encounter any rough country.

Frank 'procures' an ordnance survey map of the area from another pilot. We study it and see that Ballytain is near Donntra.

'That's about an hour, I think.'

'This auction, Frank, did you find out what time is it taking place?'

'Four o'clock but we're seeing the place at three.'

'It's ten past two, we'll never make it.'

'Oh, we'll make it Helen. Don't worry.'

14

The Cottage

HE DRIVES FAST BUT not dangerously. The roads become narrower the further along we go. The countryside is so much different here than at Cillindara. There, it is all expansive meadows and mature deciduous trees; here, it is all rocky and rugged; the meagre fields divided up irregularly by stone walls. There are sheep grazing randomly on the mountainsides. A few scattered hazels are bent over with the way of the wind. Foxgloves bloom in clumps; the yellow gorse is in flower and red fuchsias dapple the hedges. The clouds close in the sky. The sun, obscured, casts a surreal yellowed light over the land. We are cocooned. There's a soft drizzle in the air. It's the type of rain that you'd think would hardly make you wet. It is deceptive; as deceptive as the layers of intrigue that surround my mother.

As we speed along, I think again of what Charlie told me. My mother, Katherine, came from a small farm, he said. Even that I find hard to imagine. I think of her life in terms of its neatness and order. Her obsession started with beautiful clothes. She was always so insistent upon correct appearance. She would spend hours poring over fashion magazines. Once, Sybil Connelly came to dinner and my mother had fretted endlessly over what to wear. 'The Ib Jorgensen or the Chanel?'

Later on, she turned to interior design and antiques and she would take trips around the country to buy furniture. When Edgar died she commuted to Dublin and took a course in fine art and antique appreciation. It became her passion and I welcomed it, knowing that as long as she was occupied she would be more likely to leave me alone. I didn't want her interference; I wanted her out of my life completely.

Now, back in her home county, I wonder how that all came to be and her from here, the heart of the land, the very core of it. She never said it, never gave me any indication, even when I was small, that this was in her. If it was in her, it must be in me and yet she never nurtured it.

I'd say she hated it. The wildness of it wouldn't suit her. It's too raw.

Imagine what it did to her when the locals shunned her after I was born. That was what Charlie had implied. I'd say she left here with the intention of never coming back.

Charlie had said that she worked in a shop in the town: Green's Seeds and Supplies. She did the accounts, he said. Is that where she first came across the Royston family business? That would make perfect sense. It has to be the first connection between her and the Roystons. They were big suppliers of farm machinery in those days. That's what Edgar, my stepfather inherited, for all it was worth. He used to curse it. He hated the commerce of it. He almost willed it to fail. And fail it did, in spectacular fashion. Bankruptcy was common enough in the eighties and even though there was voluntary liquidation it wasn't viewed as honourable. I was too young to fully understand what was going on, but I knew that the banks had pulled the plug and the whole thing came crashing down. It was a huge comedown for my stepfather, not to be able to save the family business. There was a lot of bitterness about it at the time.

'Helen, what are you thinking? You've been quiet now for ages.'

'Oh, you know, just trying to piece it all together, that's all.'

'Do you think this house being auctioned is your mother's?'

'I don't know, and I don't know how I'm going to find out either as it's all in such a rush.'

'Maybe your mother came back down here and hid the will. What do you think?'

'Possibly; she could've done that. Then again, there's a chance she didn't. I feel I don't know anything about her anymore.'

'Oh, she's connected with it all right. I can feel it.'

'I'm not so certain.'

Silence sits with us again. Then I ask, 'What could be in it? I mean, what would be so important that someone would kidnap a child for it? That's what puzzles me.'

'It must be money or land. Isn't that what it's all about?' Frank is so confident at times and then at other times he changes. He is not comfortable now, I can sense it.

'If there is something in the will that I am due to get, something I don't know about, would you not think whoever wants it would just ask me for it? How could I miss what I didn't know I had, for Christ's sake? If that sleazeball of a guy from the train would just stay on the phone long enough I could tell him that. He can have anything; I don't care what it is, as long as I get Jack back. Anyway, I'm worried that he hasn't made any more contact.'

'Oh he will, I'm sure of it. I reckon he's watching us. We might have a couple of hours on him now with the flight, but I reckon he knows where we are.'

'Tell me how you got to be a friend of Charlie's. It would help if I really knew why you are doing all this.'

He looks at me shyly now as if I have touched on some nerve. He smiles then, a knowing smile. It's the smile that you get when you know someone is about to tell you a story, a good story. He starts talking about the summer I spent in the summer-house.

'He knew all about those parties.'

'Did he? He never said.'

'In any case,' he continues 'we knew our way around the estate long before you introduced us to it.'

'Did you? How?'

'Because,' he says, and now the smile is getting broader, 'Nick Grainger and I had been scouting around for some time for a suitable piece of land for raising crops.'

'Crops? What kind of crops?'

'Jesus, Helen, where do you think all that grass came from? We used go through a ton of it.'

'You mean you grew it on the estate?'

'That's right. We found an isolated patch of forest near the furthest end of the property, up by the river.'

'Yes, I know it.'

'We made a bit of a clearing and planted a big crop of grass there for a couple of years. No one was ever up there so we never got caught. They were none the wiser. One year, it was the second or the third season, we had a particularly good harvest. We kept all the locals supplied and even began to go further afield. We considered making a profession out it.'

I laugh at that.

'Did you make good money?'

'Ah, drinking money mostly but then again, we did a lot of drinking.'

He does that wink thing again and I smile. I wonder why I am so at ease with him. He reminds me of someone but I can't place who it is. It's got to do with his mannerisms; the way he tilts his head to you when he's talking, the way he talks at you so intently. I can't place it and it's infuriating.

'What's this got to do with Charlie?'

'Well, you see Charlie knew about it. He caught us one day up there as we were loading a couple of refuse sacks full of the stuff.'

'What did he do?'

'Nothing, absolutely nothing. That was the thing. He knew what it was and he could have gone straight to the guards. But he just told us to "finish up" and that we were well off out of it. Nothing else was ever said.'

'Did you stop growing it then?'

'Sure, we did. We were all due to go off to England to work on the sites. Charlie would have known that, in all likelihood, from talk around the town. It was the end of the summer and the crop was nearly finished. We didn't lose anything out of it. But one thing it did for me was to give me a taste for trading. Ever after, I was always looking for the fast buck or a quick deal. It gave me an eye for an opportunity, you might say, and dealing in something illegal gives you bottle. I've the nerve of a professional gambler but I only ever take calculated risks. It was my start in my business career and to tell you the truth I have no regrets. Fortunately, after that though, I was smart enough to stay on the right side of the law.'

I am amused and fascinated at this side of Frank. In the papers, when I have read about his development company, he comes across as Mr Respectable. Now that I know how he started off, and that I was part of it, I look at him in a different light. The day is one of revelation. Why are there so many aspects of my past that I never chose to see?

'That was nice of him, not to say anything, all the same. If it had been my mother who caught you it would have been a different story.'

'Oh, we were lucky for sure. After that I always looked him up when I was home. It was good of him not to rat on us. He could have got us into a lot of trouble. I always made a point of calling to see how he was … Oh holy shit!'

'What is it?'

'We have a flat. Can you not feel it? She's leaning over to your side.'

He stops the car and sure enough there is a flat tyre on the rear of the left-hand side. He opens the boot and grabs the spare. I ask him if he wants a hand but he says, no, he will be as quick himself.

I take the chance to stand outside and breathe in the different air. The soft dampness refreshes me and I throw my head back to drink it in. Through the sea air I can just about see some islands in the distance. The soft rain is mixed with a warm mist rising off the land. Within a few minutes I am soaked through. It doesn't bother me. If I allowed myself even a moment to stop worrying about Jack I think I would actually be enjoying this. It's totally quiet here and while I know I should be panicked, because we are now late for the agent, but a calmness sets in as if the pace of the land has come inside me. I am strangely at home.

Frank finishes and we continue on without being able to pick up the conversation where we left off. I would like to know more about him, Nick and Charlie, but I am too busy trying to read the ordnance survey map. I think about all the things I never knew. I wonder why my life has been so blinkered. I chide myself for being so self-obsessed.

We turn off the main road into a narrow little dirt track: a bohreen, I have heard my mother use that word. As we get nearer the base of Mount Brandon I see a small cottage nestled in underneath the mountain. It is built in such a way that you'd think it had always been there. It doesn't fight with the landscape, it blends into it, settled. It's on the shore of an inland loch. The water shines black and cold.

As we get out of the SUV the estate agent, a young girl in her twenties, comes running over to us. She looks very hassled.

'I thought you weren't coming. I've to be back in town for the auction,' she says.

We apologize and promise to spend just a few minutes looking around. From the outside it looks like a fairly traditional Irish cottage. A long structure; sort of single-storey but more like one and a half, three windows and a door to the front. The roof is going; you can see big gaps in the thatch. The walls used to be white-washed, but now are faded and little bits of moss and lichen have grown on them.

Inside, the cottage is dark and cold. There is a grey flagstone floor. In the bigger room, the living-room I suppose you'd call it, there is an open fireplace. There is a piece of rough bog oak that does as a mantle. On it there's a picture of the Sacred Heart and a black and white photo of John F. Kennedy. To the side of the hearth stand some blackened cooking cauldrons. There is a settle on one side of the fireplace and one well-worn fireside armchair on the other. It looks like it would have been comfortable in its day.

There's an old pine dresser in the next room which is the kitchen. It still holds cups and plates, mostly enamel, now rusted and chipped. The drawers of the dresser don't close properly because they are packed with papers. There is an old stove and a Belfast sink with a red and white check curtain underneath it for a cupboard. The kitchen table is a small square with a blue oilcloth tacked onto it. There are two bockedy wooden chairs and a painted baby high chair. I look at it and something about it makes me shiver.

There are two bedrooms up an open stairwell. They are divided by painted planks of tongue and grooved wood. The smaller bedroom has an old iron bedstead. The horsehair mattress is rotten.

'Looks like rats have been nesting in it,' says Frank, and I turn away in disgust.

In the larger of the bedrooms there is a painted wardrobe and a washstand with a china washing bowl and jug on it. Nailed to the wall is an unframed piece of mirror. This bedroom has an old bedstead in it too, but beside it there is a small cot with a faded bunny rabbit on it. I get a sense of *déjà-vu*. I am sure I am not imagining it. I must have been here before.

Through the cobwebbed windows I see an outside toilet. Its walls are made of corrugated iron. Beyond it lie some animal houses and a hay shed.

There is a general air of untidiness and disorganization about the place even though the cottage is practically empty. You can tell it hasn't been lived in for some while, but the odd thing is it looks like nothing has been removed since whoever owned the place lived here. It's like they left in a hurry and it has been frozen in its own time.

The estate agent is blatantly stressed and begins to whoosh us out.

'It's being sold with two acres of arable land,' she says. 'There's quite a bit of local interest. Lovely site, of course, with the lake. There are a couple of parties interested in it to use as a holiday house. The guide is three hundred and fifty thousand euro.'

'Jaysus that's steep, considering the state of the property market,' says Frank.

'A good property will always command a good price,' quips the agent. I bet she has used that phrase before.

'Who owns the house?' I ask her.

'I'm not at liberty to divulge that type of information,' and she is not to be persuaded even though I continue pressing her.

'Frank, how are we going to search this place?'

'Do you think this is your mother's house, Helen?'

'Yes. Yes, I do. It almost matches the description Charlie gave me and I just have a feeling I have been here before.'

'Let's go to the auction. We might be able to find out more there.'

15

The Auction

WE FOLLOW THE AGENT into town. It's about a twenty-minute drive. All the time I am thinking about my mother in that house. It seems so impossible that I lived there as a child with her but yet it must be true.

I try and piece bits of information together. I remember now that she was always able to swim. Does that make it definite then, that it would be her house and it beside a loch?

Then I think about her obsession with neatness and order. The cottage was in disarray. Did she react to that by going to the other extreme completely? As a child in Hill Street I remember every possession that we owned had to have its place. The scissors were in the first drawer to the left of the kitchen sink, the sewing box in the second. Winter coats to the right of the hall stand, summer jackets to the left. I was careful to maintain her system; I learned from a young age that it would be easier for me that way.

When she married Edgar and moved to Cillindara she could not stand the disorder in the Royston household. She had employed extra staff initially so that her military like system could be imposed. Her neurosis for order is one thing, but apart from that I just can't imagine her there in that isolated lonely cottage. Mrs Katherine Royston, the socialite of the district. She was forever organizing parties and dinners, charity balls and evening recitals. To me her life was one big empty social whirl.

I can't remember a day when I saw her totally alone. And she came from here? The more absurd it seems the more likely it becomes.

The question is why would she hide my father's will in that house? That's the thing that baffles me most. What would he have to leave anyway? Was Charlie right when he said Daniel was dead? If he did die in that accident, what would he, a young labourer, have to offer in his will? Maybe he's not dead at all. Is that what all this is about? I am sure Charlie knows more than he is letting on. Why exactly did he fall out with Daniel? I wish I could talk to him in person and ask more. Mostly I am worried that where I am now with Frank is not bringing me any closer to Jack. Indecisiveness hangs in the air as we arrive into Donntra.

The agent has directed us to go to the local hotel, the Imperial, where the auction is to take place. Even though the building is old, probably Victorian, it's not a pleasant place. It has a nasty smell of cabbage off it as you walk in past the main reception. You can tell that some well-meaning management did the place up in the seventies and rather than add to its original charm succeeded in ripping out any remnant of authenticity. There isn't a single original feature left. It hasn't been touched since the botched refurbishment. Everything about it is tatty. There is a conference room on the ground floor where the auction is happening. It has a dark-red carpet, white walls and drab office chairs laid out in neat rows. The room is packed. Maybe nothing much happens around here and all the locals attend each auction or perhaps there genuinely is a lot of interest in the cottage.

At the top of the room there is a table where two men are sitting. I know one of them is the auctioneer because he has a gavel in his hand, so the other must be Joseph Hayes Cunningham. I don't know who I was expecting but it wasn't him. I anticipated a man of about the same age as my mother, early sixties or so. Instead, he is in his early thirties. He is wearing a formal black suit and tie with a white shirt. His hair is dark brown and combed neatly to the side. His face is thin and there is a meanness about his mouth. I want to go and ask him the name of the vendor but as soon as we are in he starts reading out the conditions of sale. I listen and can't hear anything unusual. These are standard.

I stand at the back of the room. Frank has come in with me but I notice he quickly sidles up to someone who looks like a local leaning on one of the side walls. He begins to talk to him. The solicitor finishes reading out the conditions. The auctioneer stands and goes to a podium to the side of the desk. He begins by describing the property in glowing terms. I can hear him use words like 'outstanding site', 'vast potential', 'rural setting', but I don't hear the words in-between the phrases. My mind keeps drifting off to Jack and whether I am doing my utmost to find him. Terror begins to fill my head. A young man inadvertently bumps into me and with a jolt I realize the bidding is about to begin.

'Who will start us off with two hundred and fifty thousand for this very fine traditional property in such an excellent location?'

A hand goes up quickly from a couple in the middle of the room. The woman has a toddler on her lap. They are the holiday home type.

'Any advance on two hundred and fifty?'

'Two hundred and sixty,' comes another voice from the front.

The bidding continues to climb quickly up in tens. There are several interested parties. The auctioneer has the measure of them. Every time the bidding seems to slow he skilfully extracts another upward movement. The original couple bow out when it reaches €370,000. Disappointment is all too obvious on their faces. The auctioneer keeps going, now in increments of five thousand. I notice a man who looks like a farmer raise his hand. Another new hand goes up on my left. The room seems a lot more crowded now than when the auction began. There is a general murmur about the place that seems to be getting louder. The auction buzz has taken hold. I can't keep track of who is bidding. I don't quite understand why there is so much interest in the cottage. The price reaches 400,000 and the bidding begins to slow. I think the farmer has it.

'Any advance on four ten, any advance for this very fine property? Going once at four hundred and ten thousand euro, going twice at four hundred and ten thousand …'

He raises his gavel and is about to put it down when suddenly a voice from somewhere near the back of the room shouts out, 'Four hundred and fifty thousand.'

There is an instant silence. A hush descends the room. No one can spot who the new bid came from.

'Four hundred and fifty thousand,' says the voice again and the room begins to hum again, this time louder, with excitement.

'Any advance on four hundred and fifty thousand?' says the auctioneer who has lost some of his composure.

'Going once at four hundred and fifty, going twice at four hundred and fifty.' He taps the gavel onto the podium. 'Sold at four hundred and fifty thousand euro to the gentleman at the back. Name please?'

'Frank Callan,' comes the reply.

16

The Signing

I CAN SCARCELY BELIEVE Frank has bought the house so quickly. I am amused and stunned at the same time. The crowd begins to disperse and we make our way towards each other. For them the afternoon's entertainment is over but I have a feeling that, for us, it has only just begun. He's got a satisfied look on his face. You can tell that he's a born trader. The story about the marijuana comes back to me and I think of Frank graduating from selling dope to trading property. He was right about himself in the car.

'At least now we can get access to the place,' he explains. 'I'll tell them I want to take a few measurements for renovations or something and we can go back and give the place a good going over.'

'We still risk finding nothing and then you're stuck with the house.'

'I have a good legal team in Dublin who will get me out of it if necessary. I only have to put down forty-five grand today. It's not exactly going to break the bank,' he says.

Frank and I are asked to go into a room at the back of the auction podium to sign the contract. We are being treated as a couple by the estate agent, Johnnie Kinsella. I do nothing to dispel this impression.

Johnnie is a large man in his mid forties with a huge smile and an overly friendly manner. He won't let go of my hand and keeps congratulating us both. A beer belly extends over his belted suit trousers and his slim legs hint that once, he was thin. His nose is large and veined. His hair is a mess of light brown curls. He has abandoned his suit jacket and has rolled up his shirt sleeves. His smile is almost infectious. The auction result is obviously a good one for him.

We enter a bare room with a netted window overlooking a car-park. The solicitor sits at one side of a plain table with legal documents in piles around him. We are introduced to Joseph Hayes Cunningham. He speaks in a typically Dublin Four accent. I am confused by this. I thought that he would have some sort of Cork connection that tied him in with my mother. I expected him to be part of the Montenotte legal family for whom she worked.

I was also hoping that the owner of the cottage, or at least a rela-tive of the owner, would be in the room but there are only us four. I am disappointed. I had visualized myself walking into the room and instantly making some sort of connection. It is not going to be that easy. Thoughts that this escapade was going to bring me closer to finding Jack are fading. After the excitement of the auction I feel deflated.

Hayes Cunningham is formal in his manner and speech. His voice is without emotion; flat and soulless. He seems older and more conservative than his age. It's as if he has been a solicitor since he was a child. I can't imagine him having any connection with Jack's disappearance. He is far too upright and stiff to be involved in anything even slightly illegal.

He goes through a long list of legal documents relating to the title: land certificates, requisitions on the title and folio numbers. He is treating us like first-time buyers. Frank is just going along with it, acting as if the process of buying at auction is all new to him. I know from what I have read about Frank's company that this would be far from the truth. He's used to doing much bigger deals than this. I begin to doubt him. I become uncertain and insecure.

Hayes Cunningham produces the Contract of Sale which he says he will sign on the owner's behalf. I know that once Frank signs this document he will be committed to the purchase. I want to talk to Frank alone, about the possibility of backing out, but I can't seem to catch his eye at the right moment. He exudes confidence. I am about to ask him to step outside the room when Hayes Cunningham mentions that the sale would normally close in six weeks' time but that it might be delayed. He tries to rush through this remark and continues discussing information about the land title. Frank picks him up on it.

'Why would there be a delay?'

'It's just a precaution,' Hayes Cunningham explains. 'There was an unfortunate incident in my office where some legal documents relating to my client, the owner of the property, went … went missing. We have a full set of title deeds naturally, otherwise we would not have gone to auction.'

'That is rather unusual, don't you think? What sort of documents went missing?'

'The nature of the missing documents is confidential.'

'On the contrary. If there is a delay in closing, of course it affects me. It's the sort of thing a good solicitor would mention before the auction actually took place, don't you think?'

'I can assure you everything is in order for this transaction. I am merely being cautious and have put in a request to the land registry to ensure there were no outstanding mortgages or monies owing on the property. My client has every right to dictate the terms of this sale and this applies to how it is finally closed,' Hayes Cunningham snaps.

Nevertheless, he looks flustered. He is losing the composure he had when we first came into the room. The estate agent is getting edgy.

'I am perfectly prepared to put down a deposit on this property and have the deeds examined by my own legal team,' says Frank. 'But if there is a flaw in the title, as I am sure you are no doubt aware, the whole sale will be aborted.'

He takes up his pen as if to sign the contract and then slowly puts it down again. The tension in the room is palpable.

'We are very interested to know who actually owns this property. Helen is looking for relatives in the area. It's why we decided to buy here,' Frank continues.

'The owner is no secret,' Hayes Cunningham says. 'You have bought the property and her name can be plainly seen on the contract of sale.'

'Who is she then?' I ask, as I crane to read the legal document sideways and upside-down as it is still facing towards Hayes Cunningham.

'She is an elderly lady called Cathleen Coughlan.'

'Oh. Coughlan?'

'This is an entirely transparent transaction and that is the name that appears on the deeds.'

'Would she, by any chance, go by another name?'

'She may do, but I am under no obligation to discuss this with you. I am merely here as my client's conduit. I would have thought you'd have been well advised to have legal counsel here yourselves.'

Frank and I look at each other. I am beginning to feel lost here. What have I done? I feel responsible that Frank is buying this house and we still cannot be certain that the owner is my mother.

'Mr Hayes Cunningham,' I ask, 'do you have an office in Cork or any connection to a family of Cork solicitors?'

Hayes Cunningham looks at Kinsella in the vague hope that he will stop this interrogative tack that I am on. Kinsella is equally nervous.

'As a matter of fact I am married to a lady from Cork.'

'And her family, would they be legal people?'

'Yes, the Lynches from Montenotte. But I fail to see the relevance of my personal marital situation to your buying this property.'

I can see Frank wondering where this is going but trusting me with it. He trusts me so readily and completely. I am not used to that. The solicitor is beginning to look flustered. I decide to take a wild guess.

'Did you always handle Mrs Coughlan's affairs, or was it your father-in-law's legal firm that did it?'

'If you must know I inherited this client from my father-in-law but again I do not see the relevance of this to you.'

Now I get it. No wonder the name Hayes Cunningham meant so little to me. It was because old Mr Lynch had retired and his clients were passed on to his son-in-law Hayes Cunningham. Lynch is the name I remember Edgar mentioning when it came to legal matters. Lynch, yes, it makes sense. I can see Edgar and my mother in the big drawing-room now. I must have been about fifteen years old, home for Easter I think. Edgar is pacing up and down the room, agitated. My mother is shouting at him.

'Do you think this is why I married you, so that I could live through the disgrace of bankruptcy? I feel ashamed going out of my own front door. I can't even be seen in the village. People are talking behind our backs. I can feel it.'

'Katherine, we had no choice. I have been over this with you again and again.'

'I know you have tried to explain,' says my mother, 'but I just don't understand it. You should have listened to me before you went off ordering new equipment. I told you the firm could not afford it.'

'It wasn't just that last order. The accountant can tell you. We've been having cash flow problems for years. The bank has finally decided to pull the plug,' Edgar says. 'What we have to do now is concentrate on salvaging some sort of capital out of the business. That is our only concern.'

'We will end up paupers, on the street, not able to pay our bills. What will become of us?'

'Don't exaggerate, Katherine. It really isn't that bad. Des Lynch will see us right. He's a good legal man. He'll take care of it.'

'Yes, Des Lynch,' I say out loud to the assembled room in the Imperial Hotel in Donntra.

'Do you know him?'

'Actually he was my family's solicitor for years.'

'That *is* a coincidence I must say, Mrs Callan. I can't exactly recall dealing with you or your family on a client basis.'

I say nothing. I don't correct him as to his assumption that I am Frank's wife. I am unsure as to whether I should let him know about my Royston connection and this is good cover. Frank takes up the slack.

'The missing documents you mentioned, Mr Hayes Cunningham, would they have anything to do with a will? A will belonging to the late husband of Cathleen Coughlan?'

Hayes Cunningham now begins to get visibly nervous. The thin veneer of professional legal jargon that he has been hiding behind crumbles. He starts fumbling with his papers, as if to try and get them in order. Then he blurts out, 'The break-in at my office has nothing to do with you.'

'The break-in? You didn't mention that you had a burglary. That is a different story.'

Hayes Cunningham is furious that he has given us this information. He starts making accusations that we had something to do with the missing documents from his office. He assumes that our purchase is connected to the burglary. He is plainly very touchy about the subject. I am getting close to believing that the owner, Cathleen Coughlan, is my mother.

I haven't been able to explain the Cork connection to Frank, so he is not as certain as I am about this. The solicitor has annoyed Frank now and I notice his tone change. There is hint of malice in his voice. He points out how inconvenienced he is at the delay in closing the sale. He wonders aloud what the Law Society would think of a solicitor who goes to auction without clarifying the closing date. He is almost nasty even though his delivery is measured and controlled. I can see the ruthless streak unleashed.

Johnnie Kinsella has no idea what all this is about but he has worked out that the sale may somehow be in jeopardy.

'For God's sake man, Mr Callan bought this property in good faith. Can you just sign the contract of sale and be done with it?'

Frank takes over in a commanding manner. He shifts in his seat so he is closer to Hayes Cunningham. He stares at him and asks, 'Can you tell me if Cathleen Coughlan is your client's maiden name or her married name?'

'It is her maiden name.'

'Can you tell us her married name?'

'I told you before, I would be breaking client confidentiality if I did that.'

Frank takes out his chequebook and slowly begins to make out a cheque for the amount of €45,000. When he has signed it he holds it up and dangles it in front of Hayes Cunningham.

'It's up to you. You can have the cheque now and the sale can proceed as planned, or you can see me in court when you try to sue me for breach of contract. I wouldn't say your client will be too pleased if you go back to her with an aborted auction result and a pending legal action.'

'What is it you want?' snarls Hayes Cunningham.

'The name, the married name.'

'This is most irregular. I have never in my professional life been treated so rudely.'

'Is it Royston? Just say yes or no and we will be done with it.'

'Yes,' says Hayes Cunningham. 'It's Katherine Royston.'

17

The Search

AFTER THE SIGNING, Johnnie Kinsella wants Frank and me to go to the bar, across the road to celebrate.

'They don't do a decent pint here at all. There's a pub run by a local spinster up the main street, it's the genuine article,' he says.

I am far too anxious to waste time going for a drink and need to get back to the cottage and search it. We persuade him to hand over the keys for an hour or two and arrange to meet him later on in the pub. We drive out of town.

'You know, Frank, you realize you've just bought my mother's house. Technically I might have inherited the house anyway, when she, when—'

'When your mother dies, you mean.'

'Yes. That is the inevitable outcome, isn't it?'

'It is,' he says gently.

I haven't truly admitted that out loud yet, because the notion that my mother will be dead soon is a prospect that I don't want to deal with right now. I will get through this first, find Jack, and then I can work out what her death will mean to me. Apart from my stepfather, I have never had anyone close to me die. When Edgar died, I was devastated. For years afterwards I was lost. I cut myself off from all my emotions using anything that would blot out the pain of reality.

Edgar may have been old-fashioned and pompous, but he was a kind and devoted stepfather. He took time with me. I remember so clearly the last time I saw him. I had gone down to Cillindara to visit him for his seventy-second birthday. I hadn't seen him for three or four months and his frailness surprised me.

When my mother had first married him he was a big strong man in his middle years. To me, he had never aged, at least not until I saw him that last time. He was twenty-five years older than her and I have often wondered if that influenced my attraction to Karl. It was as if I was looking for a substitute father in my husband. It was late September and my mother had put on a small party for him in the house. I had avoided it because I had never found it easy to mingle with the Royston relations at Cillindara. I found their personal questions intrusive. Each of them had the ability to make me feel inadequate because I wasn't one of them by blood. Even though I could never accuse Edgar of treating me like an outsider, his relatives did. They made it plain by the way they spoke to me. It was something to do with the tone of what they said rather than the content. Whenever I had come back upset from one of the Royston family occasions and tried to repeat why I had been hurt or insulted to one of my friends, I couldn't explain it adequately. When I left school and went to college in Dublin I had the independence to skip family occasions altogether.

I arrived the day after the party with a present for Edgar, a new hip flask for the winter shooting season. Mother had been cross with me for not turning up the previous evening. Perhaps Edgar sensed that I would not stay long in her company so he suggested a walk around the estate. He brought his shotgun with him as he wanted to practise for the pheasant shooting. I had no interest in killing innocent birds that were bred solely for that purpose but I liked using the guns. I took the rifle. We walked around a good deal of the estate and he talked to me for the first time like I was grown up. It was as if some invisible barrier had been breached between us and now we were on a level playing field. He told me that since the bankruptcy he had been selling small bits of land off here and there so that the entire estate had shrunk from when he was a boy. He spoke about how he had always thought that the Royston land would be handed down intact from generation to generation and it was a great sadness to him that he hadn't been able to keep it that way. His biggest sadness, of course, had been the tragic death of his only son from his first marriage, but he tempered that loss with the fact that I was there with him then. We started off with a clay pigeon shoot but after a few rounds I suggested that we set up a target practise area for the rifle. I always liked the ceremonial aspect of loading the gun with individual bullets. The rifle with its polished dark wood, cold steel and shiny brass trigger seemed to me a more noble instrument than a shotgun. My idea was that if you are going to shoot something, it is better to be precise and accurate so that death comes quickly and the pain is swift and final. A shotgun death, on the other hand, where the animal is peppered with numerous small holes can cause a lingering extinction. Edgar joked when I consistently beat him and said that I had the Royston eye for accuracy.

'You could always take over the estate when your mother is gone, Helen,' he had said.

That remark had surprised me. I had never asked or expected anything from him. My mother had drilled that into me. 'Think how lucky you are that Edgar treats you like his own daughter,' she had consistently said to me. I had been fiercely independent of them both and didn't want them to feel I was an extra burden financially, so I had made a point of never taking any money from them as soon as I had left school. Edgar paid my college fees, but apart from that I supported myself completely. When he offered me the estate, it didn't, initially, make sense, but then when I thought about it, the fact that I had proved my financial independence had possibly prompted his offer. I knew he hated the thought of it all being carved up by his relatives. I didn't want to think of the legal implications of battling it out with the Royston clan, so I had dismissed the idea as impractical. My mother was only in her late forties that year so I could not envisage a time when she wasn't going to be around.

I hugged him before I left and he hugged me back tightly, reluctant to let me go. His eyes watered as I said goodbye. I drove back to Dublin feeling closer to him, feeling that we had a connection that had not been there before. In truth, I liked him more than my own mother but I couldn't admit that to myself then. The very thought of it made me feel disloyal.

I told him I would come down again soon and I meant it. I wasn't prepared for the phone call that I got a week later, telling me he was dead. I felt empty after the funeral. I was in such shock that I didn't even cry. That was a big turning point in my life. That's when I sought the anaesthetic of illegal drugs in earnest.

'Why do you think she sold it?' Frank's question brings me out of my reminiscing.

'I suppose she needs the money. That's the way my parents lived after the bankruptcy: they survived by selling things.'

'Yes, but what does she need the money for when she knows she is dying?'

'Maybe she is trying to rid herself of assets and liquidate everything, so that I have no claim to her estate. Or she could be just tidying things up. People do that before they die, you know, they like to get everything in order.'

'You will have to explain the relationship you have with your mother to me when this is all over. I don't understand it.'

There has been no further contact from the kidnapper. I decide to try and ring Madga. I have two missed calls from her but I have no signal. I ask Frank for his phone, but the signal is too weak to make a call. The lack of contact is horrendously unnerving.

At last we turn into the little bohreen that leads up to the cottage. The sky has cleared since the afternoon and a soft evening light is casting shades of red and orange over the fading landscape. Big black crows are gathering in numbers on the sparse trees that survive the stark landscape. A warmth is coming in from the hills and we wind down the windows of the SUV to drink in the last of the sunlight. Suddenly the peacefulness of the evening is shattered by the sound of a motorbike engine. As we approach the brow of the hill the bike and its rider become visible. He goes straight past us, building up speed on the downhill. Frank shouts at me to take a note of the number plate and I do my best to get it all, repeating each letter and number out loud.

'It could have been one of those scramblers,' I say, when the noise has died down.

'No, no that was a street bike. We'll go on up to the house and check it. It would be good to write the number down right away before we forget. It could be a lead. I'm sorry for shouting at you back there.'

'It's nothing; don't worry about it,' I say, but I am worried, worried about this man in whom I have so easily put my trust. With me he is soft and kind, but I am sure there is a harsher side to him.

As we near the cottage, I immediately notice the front door is open. It looks like it's been kicked in. I am hesitant when it comes to going back in, afraid that the biker might have been there and fearful of what I might find. Frank can sense it.

'Helen, there is nothing to fear.'

He seems to have a knack of saying the right thing, the soft word here, a gentle touch there. I am reassured. We both enter the house and now notice the mess. Papers are strewn everywhere, furniture has been upturned. The place has been thoroughly ransacked.

'I wonder did he find anything.'

We momentarily discuss the possibility of following the biker but both know it's too late. We painstakingly start putting the place back together.

The house looks different now that I definitely know this is where I first lived. We decide to split up for the search so Frank goes upstairs while I start in the sitting-room. There is nothing on the mantel and the picture of the Sacred Heart is lying smashed on the floor. I run my hands down behind the tattered upholstery on the fireside chair which is lying on its side. I lift the settle but can see only old newspapers. I take them out and can hardly read the print as the paper is so brittle with age. I can make out a date on one of them; 8 April 1964. It's before I was born. I move on into the kitchen and see that the contents of the dresser drawers have been emptied onto the table. There are old electricity bills, books of Green Shield stamps, Mass leaflets and the odd letter. There is nothing that looks official enough here to be a legal document. I scan the rooms again. I haven't left anything unturned. Then I look at the letters again. Some are addressed to Cathleen Coughlan and have an American stamp on them. I pick up one envelope and turn it over. It's a letter from Charlie to my mother from America; it has his address on the back of the envelope. The stripes on the edge of the envelope have been carefully slit open. Inside, the letter is written on blue airmail paper, the thin type with the consistency of tracing paper. It crackles as I open it. He used an ink pen to write and his handwriting is a delicate gothic script. Words run together a little with smudges and it makes it hard to read.

I catch phrases;

hoping all is well with you and your mother' 'reconsider Cathleen and come out here to join us' 'Me and Dan are getting on fine. There is plenty of building work here.' ... 'It's no place for you all alone there on the farm with your mother' ... 'It's time for you to leave Donntra.'

The last paragraph is easily legible;

You know you only have to say yes to the proposition I made to you and you can come out here and join me. We will only be here a couple of years, Cathleen, and then we could go home again. Please consider my offer again, Cathleen.
Your loving friend, Charlie Hegarty

So Charlie was writing to my mother but what about Daniel? Was he not writing too? I had always thought they were married before he left for America, but now I know that they weren't. Still it doesn't make sense that Charlie should write and not him. I know Charlie did not know about them being together, but it is clear he did not know about me either. Did Charlie and Daniel fall out because they both loved her?

All my life is unravelling in one day and Jack is still missing. I am being consistently bombarded with new bits of information about my past that I cannot take in. I don't know if all this is getting me any closer to finding him. Who wrote that ransom note? What do they want me to find out? How am I going to get Jack back? I take a seat at the kitchen table.

Frank comes in. He has searched the rest of the house.

'There's nothing here; the only thing I found was an old photo upstairs in the room with the cot in it. It was at the bottom of the press.'

'Show it to me.'

He hands over a faded colour Polaroid. It's of a mother and a toddler. The child is sitting on a stone wall eating an ice-cream cone. You can see a seaside beyond the wall. There are waves breaking on the beach and crowds of people. The woman is wearing denim shorts and a red halter neck top and big Blues Brother-style Raybans. A patterned scarf around her head is tied under her chin. After a second or two I recognize her as my mother. She is smiling and looking lovingly at the child. She's very young in it. She's very beautiful in it. I never saw that quality so strikingly in her before but I see it in this faded photo. The child must be me. I look so happy dangling my legs over the wall, looking up to my mother. She looks happy too, happy just because she is with me. I can't imagine that day at all although the photograph tells me that it existed. There was a day then, at least one day, where I was happy to be with her and she with me.

I take the photo from him and show him the letter. We agree to have another look around to see if there is anything else that we have missed. After an exhaustive search we do not find a will. Frank has even looked in the sheds. We decide to go back into town and go and talk to Kinsella; we have to give the key back anyway, and now I need that drink. We drive again, back to Donntra.

'I can't believe it, where does my father fit in? Why are there no letters from him? Maybe that's why Charlie and he fell out, over my mother. He said so, of course. They were both interested in her. Maybe she took Daniel's letters with her because they meant more to her. Is that it?'

'I can't answer you, Helen. I don't know.'

'I'm just thinking out loud that's all.'

I am teasing out the possibilities in my head when my thoughts are interrupted by my phone ringing. It's Madga.

'Helen, thank God. I have been trying to reach you.'

'I've been out of coverage. Is there any news?'

'First I couldn't get hold of Karl's solicitor for ages. Then when I did the guards refused bail.'

'They did *what*?'

'They refused bail on account of him already having a drugs record.'

'Oh, Jesus.'

'Yes, exactly. But you know the paintings? The ones the guards said were stolen?'

'Yes, what about them?'

'They are from your mother's house.'

'What? How could that be?'

'Karl is claiming that your mother gave them to him to sell.'

'I didn't know he had any contact with her. Surely he would have told me?'

'Your mother reported three paintings stolen and has made an insurance claim for them.'

'Christ, why does she need to raise money so badly that she had to ask Karl to sell them and make an insurance claim on them? Is she effectively selling them twice? Who is telling the truth here?'

'It appears Karl is. There have been phone calls back and forth to Charlie. Apparently your mother made a mistake. Charlie is claiming mental confusion due to illness. Your mother is so delirious now that it would be impossible to get any sense out of her.'

'This is totally bizarre. She has just sold her original family home, to Frank, as it happens. What does she need all the cash for?'

'I don't know, Helen, but it looks like Karl won't get out until Jack has made an appearance. I'm still here by the way, in your house. I stayed here most of the afternoon just in case, you know, in case the kidnapper made contact.'

'And did he?'

'No, Helen, there's nothing yet.'

She asks about Frank and the house and I fill her in. I say goodbye and agree that she will ring me as soon as we hear anything.

Frank has overheard the whole conversation so there is no need to go over it with him. It is incredible that my mother got Karl to sell paintings for her. He must have known she was ill. Why didn't he tell me?

'So Karl did time?' asks Frank.

'Oh, yes, two years in Mountjoy, for possession. Fortunately he didn't have enough on him to make the "intent to supply" charge stick. He could have got a lot longer.'

'When was this?'

'Years ago. I had just got pregnant with Jack. He didn't get out till Jack was fifteen months old.'

'So you were pregnant and had Jack on your own?'

'Yes.'

'Did anyone help you? What about your mother?'

'My mother? She would be the last person I would tell for fear of what she would make me do. I had a few close friends who stood by me.'

'For fear of what?'

'Nothing, it's just a turn of phrase.' Christ almighty I think how did that come out? I don't want Frank to know everything about me and the way he seems to be finding out so readily is disturbing. I am too exposed. I don't know enough about him.

'I never knew that; I never knew you were on your own,' he says. He leaves me puzzled because he seems genuinely concerned.

I am grateful when we reach Donntra and I can end this conversation.

18

The Pub

WE PARK AND WALK up the main street and find the pub where Johnnie said to meet. We enter a dimly lit square room. On one side of it there is a bar and on the other side there is a shop with all sorts of odds and sods for sale; Wellington boots, tins of baked beans, clothes pegs and bread. I didn't know there were any of these types of pubs left intact. There are a few stools on the bar side and a snug tucked up at the back. A couple of mismatched wooden chairs and tables are scattered in the centre of the room. At the back of the pub there is a further doorway with a multi-coloured curtain made out of plastic strips. Past the doorway is the entrance to someone's private home.

As we get accustomed to the dark lighting inside we are greeted by Johnnie Kinsella. He is in great form and everyone in the pub seems to know him. His humour is no doubt helped by the high price he achieved for the cottage. I imagine he has already added up the commission in his head. I notice his nose seems to have got redder since the afternoon and wonder how many pints of Guinness he has downed in the interim. He keeps introducing us as the 'couple who bought the Coughlans' place, Frank and Helen.'

We order drinks and join him at the bar. He wants to know all about us; what we plan to do with the house; how often we will be down here; why we decided to buy after only seeing it once. He doesn't let up with his questions. It is awkward and I am not good at making up false stories. I am painfully honest but now, in this situation, I am also evasive.

I gulp down a gin and tonic, served up by a young-looking local lad, and fidget with some beer mats. Frank starts talking about the renovation possibilities of the cottage with a practised builder's eye. Thankfully, he and Johnnie get technical and I have an excuse not to join in.

I look around the room and see a motley clientele. There are a couple of locals and a smattering of Dublin accents, holidaymakers, I expect. There are some blatant Americans, recognizable by their almost identical clothes of windcheaters, chinos, and brand-new white trainers. I don't know how you can wear trainers for more than a day without scuffing them. I think of Jack's Golas and how wrecked they are. He wears them every day after school and all weekend when he's on his skateboard. I had promised I would buy him a new pair. It's a promise I have got to keep.

I begin to get more anxious with every passing minute. Is there not something else I could be doing to get Jack back besides sitting in a bar drinking gin and tonic? I begin to question my decision not to be straight up with the guards. If I had told them the truth they could be out searching for him now. But where would they start? I don't know if he is still in the country, let alone which part. I don't think we are going to find out anything here that will be of any help to finding Jack. I want to go back to Cillindara and talk to Charlie. He must have a lot more information about when my mother and he were younger. Surely he can fill in some gaps.

I can hear Frank asking Johnnie Kinsella about who instructed him to sell the house.

'All my instructions were through that solicitor, Hayes Cunningham. I never met anyone else at all in connection with the property. Sure you had the measure of him anyway, I'll give you that. That jackeen scurried off like a rabbit wounded by a fox after you two left.' He breaks off into spontaneous laughter.

This mood does not suit me at all and I am about to ask Frank to leave when, from behind the plastic curtain, an elderly lady makes her entrance. She is dressed formally in a bottle-green crocheted suit, is wearing full make-up; orange lipstick, brown eyeliner that not been applied too accurately and mascara. Three strands of purple glass beads adorn her neck. She has matching purple drop ear-rings and her ear lobes are being pulled down with the weight of them. She is small, about five foot two, and has her hair tied back softly, with a velvet ribbon in it. I can see hints of light auburn amidst her grey strands. She stands momentarily in front of the plastic curtain commanding attention. There is a polite silence. Satisfied that she is noticed, she smiles and makes her way around the room, greeting people individually. She comes over to us.

'Allow me to introduce you to your hostess, Julia Coughlan,' Johnnie says. *Coughlan* is she a relative of my mother's then is my first thought? Her eyes lock on mine and stay there a few seconds too long for it to remain comfortable. She insists on giving us a drink on the house. As she goes behind the bar I watch her movements. They are slow, measured, and thought out. I am wondering what age she is, maybe in her seventies, when Johnnie whispers to me, 'They say around here that Julia is eighty-five.'

She pulls half of the men's pints and leaves them to settle. With painstaking care she pours my gin into a measure and then on into an ice-cubed glass. She cuts and adds a slice of lemon. Then she free pours an extra drop of gin into the already measured glass. She sees me watching.

'I always give a local a little extra,' she says.

I am astounded. She goes back to the pints and finishes them off, all the time making small talk with Frank and Johnnie.

I can feel her eyes on me while she is talking. What did she mean a local? As Frank and Johnnie continue to talk Julia asks me, 'Have you been here before? You look very familiar. I never forget a face.'

I am not sure how I should answer. All I can say is, 'I can't remember.'

I finish my drink quickly and feel light-headed. I remind myself that I haven't eaten anything all day. I must go pale because the next thing I am aware of is Julia asking me if I am feeling all right.

'Would you like to come into the back with me and have a cup of tea while the gentlemen finish their drinks?'

I get up and follow her through the striped plastic curtain. Behind the curtain is more dim light. It's a sort of kitchen and sitting-room all in one. There is a small stove to one end and she puts the kettle on it and begins to assemble china cups and saucers. They have a pattern of crimson roses and a rim of gold around the edges. I only notice this as I am standing so self-consciously beside her.

As we are waiting for the kettle to boil Julia stares at me again. She takes my wrist and bids me to come over to the window where there is still some fading remnants of evening light. She looks earnestly into my face, searching for something. After a few moments, she relaxes and smiles.

'Now I have it, I'm sure of it, you're Cathleen's daughter, aren't you? Helen, Helen Coughlan.'

'I don't go by the name Coughlan. But it is my mother's maiden name. Am I related to you in some way?'

She ignores my question and asks, 'What name do you go by now?'

'My name is Helen Rafferty'

'Really, is that so? Is that your married name?'

'It is.'

'And tell me, girleen, what was your name before you got married?'

'It was Royston for a time and then before that it was Fitzgerald.'

'Ah, Fitzgerald. That would make sense. She was always clever, Cathleen, I'll give her that.'

'What do you mean?' I ask, and I show a brief flash of anger, sparked by this stranger knowing who I am and getting at my mother all in the space of sixty seconds.

'Sure now, there's no doubt in my mind at all, girleen. You have her temper.'

'Look, suppose I am Cathleen Coughlan's daughter. What can you tell me about her? Did you know her?'

Julia smiles and ignores my question. She is in control of this conversation. That much is evident.

'You took a long time coming back, didn't you? Not that I blame you, you understand. I wouldn't have been surprised if you never came back here at all.'

'Why do you say that?'

'Cathleen, she wasn't treated well around these parts. Not after you were born. After your grandmother's funeral she packed up, closed the door of that cottage and swore she'd never come back. You understand it was different times then, different times.'

'Tell me about her, please, I need to know.'

'A girl needs to know about her own mother?'

'She's never talked about her life down here to me. Please, I have to know.'

'Cathleen and I are related. Her grandfather was my grandfather's brother. That makes us second cousins. That's how she got the job, you see. The job in the farm supply shop. Surely she has told you all this?'

'I knew she worked in a shop.'

'Green's was the shop, it was next door. It's long gone now.'

'So what about her job in the shop? Did something happen there? Is that why you are telling about it?'

Julia looks at me again intently. I feel she can see all the way through me.

'Tell me, why did you come down here and buy the house? Why is she selling it after all this time? Wouldn't you be getting it anyway? Aren't you her only child, her only surviving relative?'

'It's complicated, Julia. I can't explain it now. Can you just tell me about my father, about Daniel Fitzgerald?'

'Daniel, your father? Oh Lord God, girleen, it isn't my place to be telling you about your own father.'

She holds on to the stove and sits down in a chair beside it. The kettle has boiled and she slowly gets up again and makes the tea. I want to hurry her up and ask her more questions, but I sense that I am on Julia-time here and will have to wait for her to continue. She pours out the milk first, smiling at me all the while, and then the tea from the warmed pot. Finally after what seems like an interminable length of time she asks, 'What makes you think Daniel Fitzgerald is your father, Helen?'

'Because my mother told me. How else would I know?'

'Daniel went to America to work with Charlie Hegarty and his brothers.'

'Yes, I know that.'

'Charlie, Daniel and your mother were great friends before they went. There's many that thought she would go with one of them. But not Cathleen. She had set her sights on higher things. She stayed on at the shop.'

'Why?'

'To look after her own mother for one thing and then again …' She pauses; her eyes dart around the room as if she is checking whether anyone is listening. She looks almost afraid to go on. I stand up close to her and stare at her directly.

'Julia, whatever you know you have to tell me. My son, my only son, Jack, is in great danger and I have to find my father's will to save him. Please help me, Julia, please.'

I can feel the tears well up in me. I am trying to stop them but the plug that I have put on them since this morning has come loose. My crying starts softly and then the tears just flow with no noise at all. They just keep flowing until my face is flooded and through the murkiness I can see Julia crying too.

She reaches out and takes my hand again and this time she whispers, 'Your mother,' she says, 'your mother stayed here when those boys went off to America. She had you over a year later, over a year. Daniel wasn't your father; she may have claimed that when she moved away, she was clever enough to make his death a convenience to her, but I swear to God Almighty he wasn't your father.'

'Who was then? Who was it, Julia?'

'Do you know why the people gave her such a hard time of it around here? Do you not know that if he had been a local they would have maybe been a bit kinder to her? A wedding would have been arranged by any decent family. No, your father was not from around these parts. Your father was a married man, Helen, a married man and a Protestant at that.'

'Julia, who are you talking about?' I hold onto the stove for support. I know what's coming.

'I'm talking about the man she met through the shop, the man who owned the big farm supply firm.'

'You mean Edgar, don't you? Edgar Royston.'

Through my tears I see her nodding in agreement.

19

The Run

AS I RUN FROM the kitchen and go back through the pub the realization that Edgar is my real father completely overwhelms me. There is a battle going on in my head. One voice is telling me that it can't be true, and another is scolding me, telling me that it plainly is and that it's a wonder I never pieced it together before.

Frank catches my eye and sees that I am alarmed. He raises his hands, palms up towards the ceiling in an open gesture and mouths 'what's up' silently, but I ignore him. I see the door; take it out to the street, and start running. I sprint all the way up through the town as if my life depended on it. I have no idea where I am headed. I have to get away from all this.

My confusion turns to anger. *She* hid this from me all her life. I can understand her reluctance to tell me before they got married – I was too young – but why couldn't *she* have told me afterwards? And what about Edgar? What was his excuse for never saying anything? Was that what he was hinting at the last time I saw him?

I wonder who else knew that I was his natural daughter and if this has something to do with Jack. Of course it has. Frank was right all along. I keep running in the hope that this burst of physical energy will make the revelation about my true parentage comprehensible.

From nowhere the picture of the junkie at the train station comes into my head. For one quick second I think it would have been nice to score, even after all these years; score and find oblivion. I haven't touched a drug since that night before the bust, but now I don't want to face reality. I want to pass into a lovely darkness for a few minutes, a few hours. Blankness will get me away from all this pain. All these years I have kept it together for Jack. He was my only reason to stay clean. All these years and now I know the core of my addiction has never left me. I have suppressed it, controlled it, tried to ignore it and now, when I need all my resolve and strength, the demon comes back to burden me, to take me over again, to ruin the only thing that I have ever cared about: my son Jack.

The thought of going back to the pub and downing a couple more gin and tonics holds strong attraction for a few moments. I could get Julia to give me doubles and drink until I am past caring. But I know that's not true. I couldn't do that. I care too much, but I could fool myself into not feeling anything. I keep running, welcoming the chill wind that blows up erratically around me. I maintain the sprinting pace until I get to the outskirts of the town. The road is dark and narrowing. My sense of orientation is confused. I stop only because I am winded. I bend over in a gateway and, breathless, let my head fall between my knees. As I try to recover all I can think about is Edgar, Edgar my father. It sounds strange even as I say it to myself.

Edgar. All this time I have been thinking about my mother and finding out about her past, when I should have been concentrating on him. Edgar, my father, it *does* make sense. It has to be true. It explains my mother's marriage to him. Of course, he had no other heir after his son died and passing on his bloodline was almost an obsession with him. It could explain the resentment of his relatives towards me. If only they had told me, I could have understood so much more.

This changes things, it changes things utterly. My attention goes back to the note. I fumble about in my jeans pocket for it.

Your father's will is lost. We know that it is hidden in a house that you lived in when you were young.

My father is Edgar. I have to accept that. ... *hidden in a house that you lived in when you were young*. Julia said Mother never came back. That the house had been abandoned the day after my grandmother's funeral. If she never came back here, then the will must be somewhere in Cillindara. That's the only thing that would make sense. It must be in Hill Street, or in the main house. I have to get back there, I have to find it. I wonder if it was a coincidence that made me come to Donntra and uncover my true heritage, or perhaps it was part of someone else's plan.

My breathing returns to normal and I lift my head up to see where I am. The darkness has crept in while I was running. Cloud cover obscures the stars. I have lost my bearings and cannot see any town lights.

I start walking downhill in the hope that I am going in the right direction. My mobile rings. The shrill sound in the silence of the country startles me. It's Karl.

'Helen, where the hell are you?'

'Where am I? I'm looking for Jack. Where the hell do you think I am? Why don't you start explaining things, Karl? What were you doing with my mother's paintings? Were they stolen, or were the two of you up to something illegal together? You knew she was sick and you left it up to Charlie to tell me. What exactly is going on here? Where are you calling from? Why aren't you still locked up?'

'I'm out on bail, charges are pending. It's too complicated to explain now but your mother gave me the paintings to sell. You have to believe me.'

'What has this got to do with Jack? Why was he taken? I swear to God, if it's anything to do with you and if anything happens to my son, I'll kill you.'

'Stop exaggerating.'

'I am not exaggerating, Karl, I'm perfectly serious.'

There is a noticeable silence on the line and I fear that I have lost the signal. I walk back the way I came. When Karl speaks again, it's softer, more polite, as if he has realized he is treading on dangerous ground.

'You've got to get back to Cillindara. I have a lot to tell you.'

'What is it? Tell me now.'

'No. Not like this. I have to explain the past to you in person.'

'What are you talking about? Stop fucking around with me Karl and tell me whatever it is now.'

'I can't explain everything to you over the phone. I knew your mother before I met you. I should have told you a long time ago.'

'What? How did you know her? Why did you never tell me?'

'It's too complex. Please wait until I can see you in person. I'm sorry about everything, but believe me, I had nothing to do with Jack being taken. It's all to do with what you are due to inherit.'

'Inherit? I was due to inherit nothing. I don't understand any of this.'

'It's too intricate for you to understand; there are a lot of issues to be resolved here. I need to meet you at Cillindara.'

Too intricate for me to understand? That patronizing bastard.

'Issues? You're calling the disappearance of your son a goddamn issue? What are you doing out of custody anyway? I thought they would hold on to you until Jack turned up.'

'That's the other reason I'm ringing. He did. At least we think he did.'

'What? Oh my God why didn't you tell me this straight away? I am demented with worry. Is he all right?'

'No, Helen, it's not like that. A kid turned up at the Garda station in Cillindara just after six o'clock. Charlie walked right into the station with him, claimed it was Jack, and colluded with the story we had given that Detective O'Meara earlier.'

'A kid? Was it Jack?'

'I don't know. All I know is that the guards think the issue of his disappearance is closed now. They are off our backs.'

'I was the one who told Charlie all about the guards. I spoke to him from my house earlier on.'

'I know, Magda told me, and we have deduced that you gave him the information.'

He has my hackles up with this remark.

'Don't put this back on me, Karl. Ring him and find out what's going on.'

'That's the problem, we have been trying non-stop since I got out of custody, but he is completely out of contact. He, or anyone else, won't answer the phone down there.'

'I can't believe Charlie had anything to do with this. He was so upset this morning. It doesn't make sense.'

'I suspect he is being coerced. But it does mean that he must have some contact with the kidnappers.'

'Are the guards happy that this boy who turned up is Jack? Did the photograph that I gave them match the description of this boy?'

'That's the thing; my lawyer, Giles, overheard a conversation at the station. Apparently the local Garda station in Cillindara doesn't have a working scanner or fax so they weren't able to match the photo. He was a teenager for sure, with red hair like Jack's, and seeing as Charlie knows the local guards he got away with it. In any event they had to let me go after Charlie backed up my story.'

'I'll meet you in Cillindara as soon as I can.'

'I'm going to try and ensure I am not being followed, so I may have to take a circuitous route. Have you received any more calls from the kidnapper?'

'No, nothing.'

'I hope you made the right decision; not telling the guards and trusting that complete stranger, Frank.'

'Frank isn't a stranger, for your information, and I am making the best decisions I can under the circumstances. If you want to turn this into a fight go right ahead, but I think our priority should be finding Jack, not bitching at each other.'

'Very well, I hear you.'

'Stay in touch by phone if you hear anything else.'

'Understood. I'll meet you when I get to Cillindara.'

There are so many more things going on here than I understand. With each passing second I am getting more and more confused. I need so many answers. I have to believe that it was Jack who turned up at the Cillindara Garda station. Any other possibility is too difficult for me to think about. I close my eyes and try and picture getting my Jack back but horrible images come into my head of him being tied up in a darkened room, of him not being able to move, and being frightened, and crying and wondering why I am not there with him. The images won't go away and they keep getting more and more terrifying.

Forcing myself to open my eyes and look around I see a glimmer of lights from the town. The sound of a car engine breaks the stillness of the night. It's Frank. I don't know how he found me considering that I hardly know where I am myself. He gets out of the car.

'Ah, there you are. Did you feel like a bit of fresh air? I wouldn't mind a bit of a walk myself.'

20

The Accident

HE KNOWS THERE HAS been some kind of development but I think he is too sensitive to ask me outright. All this information is too much for me to handle. I start shaking uncontrollably. I think I am going to have a panic attack. I haven't had one since I first got off the junk. They always start off like this, the shaking, then the sobbing; I have already got to that stage. My breathing is too fast. I know if I don't slow it down I will start hyperventilating and I could faint. I am waiting for my body to begin to start rocking uncontrollably. After that the paralysis will follow; it will creep up my body slowly making each of my limbs immobile. My legs will go first, one at a time and then my stomach and each of my arms. When the immobility reaches my chest I will be rigid with fear. I can't have this happen now. '*I must take control and stop this,*' I keep telling myself but the more I try to control it the more it progresses. I can feel the numbness coming on.

Frank moves closer to me and I let him put his arms around me in a hug. He can sense my hysteria. His grip gradually becomes firmer, safer. It's almost as if he knows what's happening to me. He wipes away my tears with his hands.

'We're going to find him,' he says over and over.

I am still shaking but less now. That comfortable familiar quality that I have with him is back. I still can't place it. I am more aware of it when I am physically close to him. He is gentle and strong at the same time. My vulnerability diminishes and I feel protected.

Even the smell of him is reassuring. He keeps wiping away my tears and now he is kissing my cheeks. It feels natural for me to let him find my mouth and kiss him back. I want to feel the touch of someone who cares. With each kiss it feels like he is calming me. I want to go on and connect with him and let him caress me but I stop.

I can't do this, not now. The moment finishes as quickly as it started and we both take a step back from each other, embarrassed, lost for words.

'I'm sorry, I don't know what came over me,' he's saying.

I gather myself together slowly. My breathing has settled now. The images of a frightened Jack have left my head.

'Don't worry about it. Maybe we can talk about it later. Right now we've got to get back to Cillindara. What's the quickest way? Can we get back to Faranfore and fly?'

'No, it's too dangerous. My licence doesn't cover me to fly at night. Besides, there's no airstrip at Cillindara unless we land in a field, which can be tricky at the best of times, but in the darkness it's too risky. In any case the hangar at Faranfore will be locked up by now. We'll have to drive. We should be able to make it in two and half to three hours.'

'OK, let's go. I'll fill you in on the way.'

We leave town in the dark of the night. I have lost track of time. I tell Frank about my father. 'I knew it; I knew this whole thing was to do with him.' I recount the story of a teenager turning up at the Garda station with Charlie. 'No way has Charlie anything to do with this. He's being forced into it for sure,' he says.

We start trying to tease out the implications of my true heritage. We agree that me being a true Royston means that none of the extended Royston family will benefit from the estate. This certainly gives them a motive to take Jack. Somehow though, this notion of the Roystons being involved in criminal activity to get money does not sit well with me. It wouldn't be their natural instinct. From what I can remember they are all reasonably well off in any case.

I am getting more and more agitated again. I just keep looking at my watch and wishing away the time till we get back to Cillindara.

Frank pulls over suddenly and stops the engine. He gets out and takes off his coat.

'Look, you'd be better off lying down in the back and trying to get some rest. You're making me nervous driving. You've been up since dawn and this whole thing isn't over yet. You need to stop and be quiet for a while. Just try it, Helen.'

I reluctantly agree and move into the back seat. I am convinced I will never sleep, but I welcome the silence. I have been talking around in circles with Frank for easily an hour. I need to think. I find myself fighting the desire to sleep but the constant motion and the soundless space that I am in makes me drowsy. I close my eyes and surprise myself by falling into a sort of half-sleep. Part of me is still aware of the car moving along the road and some other part of my brain is dreaming up images from my past; the shooting expedition with Edgar, the parties with the Roystons, the fighting with my mother that went on all of my life. Images of faces keep surfacing in my head: Edgar's sister, Eliza, her ghastly husband, Nigel, the staff on the estate, inconsequential people whom I haven't thought about in years.

Then images of long forgotten faces fade away and now I see my mother prancing up and down in her new replica Victorian conservatory. She's wringing her hands and speaking in that horrible, angry sarcastic voice of hers. It's the one I swore I would never use and yet, there are times when I have got very cross with Jack and, to my horror I have heard that same voice in me.

'Calm down, Katherine,' Edgar is saying.

'Calm down? What's there to be calm about when my only child comes back from boarding-school in a state like this?'

Edgar is standing in front of me while I cower in the corner. It is the first time I remember having a feeling that he cared for me more than she did. I had never understood why my mother had married him. I thought he was old enough to be my grandfather. It embarrassed me when he came to the school sports day and people asked me who he was. On top of that I had blamed him for sending me away in the first place.

I was always in trouble in boarding-school, but the year I finished school was definitely the worst kind of trouble I had ever been in. I had hated leaving Cillindara and couldn't settle in any of the schools they sent me to. It was in the eighties and being Irish wasn't yet fashionable in England. Nobody had been directly cruel to me but it was obvious that I didn't fit in with the other English girls. I went from being top of the class in my local primary school to being a middling low achiever in the English system. I had never studied French or English history like the others but nevertheless Edgar and my mother had expected me to adapt without trauma.

I engineered getting expelled from the first two schools by breaking every rule I could think of. I reasoned that if I kept getting thrown out Edgar and my mother would relent and let me go back to school in Ireland. God how I had hated being sent away. I felt as if I was being punished for something that I didn't do. I frequently ran away and tried to get back home. Once I made it on the Old Mail boat all the way to Dun Laoghaire but Edgar had arrived and persuaded me to go back.

'You need a good start in life and that's what a British education will do for you,' he had reasoned.

And so I had conceded to his wishes and tried to settle down. I stopped running away, but I still couldn't behave like a model student. My wild streak had been too well established and I had a reputation to uphold with those uptight English girls. They expected me to be wayward and, my God, I was. I was constantly in detention for some infraction of the school rules. My sole aim was to be as outrageous as possible.

My third boarding-school, Brookville, was near Brighton and as I was in sixth form we were given a little more freedom. The fact that we were allowed into town on Sundays and the prospect of this being my last year in England combined to make me slightly happier than I had been before. I even began to form friendships. Samantha was from London and her parents had sent her to

Brookville as a last resort in the hope that she would get enough A levels for admission to a reasonable English university. We had a lot in common; her mother had recently remarried, an older man too, and she was an only child. We became best friends.

She knew a crowd of students from the art college and one night we had skipped out to a student party. It was held in a flat in Havelock Square. The building itself was run down and inside all the rooms were painted dark red. Belongings were strewn around the floor and abstract paintings with a surreal quality were propped up against the walls. One of the students must have been a Munch fan because there were several look-a-likes of *The Scream*. The kitchen sink was full of weeks old, filthy crockery. The flat itself was made up of a warren of little rooms and the whole place was tremendously dark, disorganized and confusing.

When we arrived, Samantha soon hooked up with her boyfriend and immediately disappeared into a bedroom. I was left with a crowd of strangers, not that it bothered me.

We had brought half a bottle of vodka and Samantha had left it with me. I went looking for a glass or a reasonably clean cup and came across a group of guys who looked interesting. After a couple of swigs of vodka I mustered up enough courage to inveigle my way into their conversation. They were having a heated discussion about the coal miners' strike and the right wing politics of Margaret Thatcher. I joined in with my views on Bobby Sands and the struggle for a United Ireland. I held strong political views, bordering on the socialist, and I could carry an argument well.

I shared the rest of the vodka with them and then somebody produced a whole bottle of tequila. It wasn't long before a joint appeared. I had never had hash before but I was all on to try it. I was having a good time. This is what cool grown ups did, I told myself. One of the boys introduced himself as Anthony, and engaged me in a more personal conversation. After a time the group dispersed and Anthony and I were left alone. The music got louder and part of the room was cleared and turned into an impromptu dance floor. We started dancing and when the music slowed he held onto my waist. He kept his hand there when the track had finished. I was comfortable with him and didn't make any attempt to stop him leading me to a couch and kissing me. It got late and I couldn't find Samantha. I was beginning to feel sick from the alcohol and wanted to leave, but Anthony insisted that he would find Samantha for me. He led me to a darkened bedroom. He started kissing and caressing me and I told him to stop. I needed to get back to school before we were found out, but the alcohol weakened my resolve. I was softer. I didn't realize how much I needed a human touch. My mother had never been physically affectionate and I grimaced when I was made to kiss Edgar on the check. A longing was unleashed once Anthony's hands touched my skin. I tried to fight it. I tried not to give into him but as soon as he had started I didn't want him to stop. He felt good and I felt ready. I wanted him to touch me all over, to make me feel special, loved, desirable. He kept telling me I was beautiful and I needed to believe him. There was another part of me that wanted to go back into the dorm and brag about this to all those prissy little bitches.

It was all over quickly. I never saw Anthony again after that night. I was completely mixed up about him. Did I encourage him? Should I have done it? Why did I need it so much? I felt cheap and used the next day and for many days after. Intimacy on that level was not something that I was capable of. The girls in the school dorm didn't find out from me. Somehow I had a feeling I had gone too far this time. When the morning sickness started I knew that my life would be forever changed because of what I had done that night.

When I came home at the end of term my mother had picked up on it straight away. I can still hear her exact words in the conservatory.

'And who's the father? I don't suppose a little slut like you even knows. Fancy sending you off to an expensive boarding-school like Brookville and you coming back knocked up. Isn't that what they call it these days? You're nothing but a common whore. What did they think you were over there? A bloody Irish slag?'

'Don't speak to the child like that. She needs our support,' Edgar pleaded.

Venomous would be a kind word to describe her mood that day.

'The disgrace of it. Can you imagine what the staff would say if they found out? We are pillars of this community. Can you not understand that people look up to us and expect us to lead by example? How are you going to start art college when you are three or four months pregnant? Well, have you any answers, girl?'

'You were young once yourself, Katherine,' Edgar had said.

That remark had really got her going. Now, of course, I understand why.

'I don't know what you are implying, I most surely don't. Get her out of my sight and make arrangements to get rid of that bastard she is carrying.'

'I'm not having an abortion, Mother. You can't make me do that.'

She went for me then as if to hit me and I ran out of the conservatory and up the stairs. She came after me shouting that I was an ungrateful little bitch. She was completely out of control. As I continued up the stairs she grabbed at my leg. I stumbled. I toppled over and fell backwards. I rolled all the way to the bottom of the stairs. My mother continued shouting and Edgar began to shout back at her. I remember it all now. Words that I had chosen to forget.

'You think I'm going to let you tell her now? This girl isn't fit to know her own heritage.'

'Stop it, Katherine. Don't bring this up now. Can't you see she's hurt?'

'Oh my God, there's blood everywhere,' was the last thing I remember my mother saying.

I think again about Edgar. I remember him being so kind to me after 'the accident' as he referred to it. He came to my room and sat with me while he read from his favourite novels. When I tried to talk about the baby I had lost he only shushed me. It was the closest we ever got. If only he had told me he was my real father then I could have loved him better.

I shiver myself awake and am amazed at how long I have managed to put that scene out of my life. I have literally never thought about it. A piece of me cut my mother off entirely after that. Whatever she subsequently did to try and regain my affection made absolutely no difference to me. The door to my emotions for her was always firmly shut. That's why I never told her I was pregnant with Jack. I waited until he was born. I wasn't going to put up with her disapproval again.

I jump up in surprise when Frank says, 'The tank is nearly empty. I'm going to pull over up here.'

I see an all night garage come into view. Frank gets out and starts to fill up. I spend a few moments gathering myself together and realize we have been driving for over an hour and a half.

I get out of the car, feeling washed out and not at all refreshed from sleeping. My offer to Frank for petrol money is refused.

'Frank, don't think I'm going to stitch you for the forty-five grand or anything, I'll sort you out for it.'

'I'm not worried about money, that's the last thing that concerns me.'

I go into the shop and grab some drinks and chocolate to keep me going. I think about offering to drive. Frank must need a break at this stage. I go to the toilet and throw water on my face from the basin. The towel is too dirty to use and there is no toilet roll left. I search my pockets for a tissue and find a piece of paper. I have it taken out before I realize that I'm still wearing Frank's coat. I stare at the coloured pencil image for a few seconds before I realize what it is in my hands.

It's a drawing of two bikes, one red and the other black thrown up on a pavement, at an angle, as if to deliberately block pedestrians. I recognize Tommy's style immediately. He has pencilled in the word 'Yamaha' on one of petrol tanks. The two young men he has put beside them, at first do not seem to have any unusual features. One has short-cropped fairish hair and an innocent-looking grin. The other has neck-length brown locks and darker eyes. He's drawn in every other detail: the railway crossing, some passers-by, a car parked on double yellows. It's Sydney Parade DART station without any doubt. It's where Jack and Tommy always get the train home from school. I stare at the drawing, particularly at the darker guy. Then I notice a little scar mark over his left cheek. Yes, after a few seconds I am sure of two things: one that the black bike is the one that was at the cottage and that the young man with the darker features and the scar is the boy from the train – Derek.

21

The Drive

MY HAND SHAKES INVOLUNTARILY as I carefully refold the paper and put it back into Frank's pocket. I leave it the way I found it.

The layers of intrigue are confounding me. He knew we were looking for the drawing when we were in my house. It isn't an accident that it ended up here, in his pocket. He must have taken the drawing and hidden it from me so that I wouldn't recognize Derek. Why would he be intentionally deceitful? I begin to think there is a possibility that he is working with the kidnapper. Why else would he be so generous with his time and money?

A little while ago I thought that he held some genuine affection for me, that Jack and I mattered to him. Throughout the day I had come to believe that he sincerely felt for me; that he had an affinity with me in a way that made us close. For Christ's sake I even told him about my father. He knows almost as much as I do about my past. I feel exposed and horribly raw in front of him. Finding Tommy's drawing means that I can't trust him. I can't trust anyone. There is only me. I am alone.

I think what could be happening to Jack, right now, at this very moment and I am powerless to help. I am caught in a web of lies and deception that I can't make sense of. I feel nauseous. I vomit in the sink.

Subdued and confused I walk back to the car. Frank is all ready to get going but he can sense a change in me. He continues driving.

'How long more do you think it is?' I ask.

'Oh only another hour or so,' he says.

He tries to needle me for more information about Edgar and the estate, but I am not biting. I have lost my easiness with him. He puts his hand on my arm, asks, 'What's up? Something happened to you back there at the station. Did you get a call from the kidnapper that you're not telling me about? You're different.'

I pull back from his touch wanting to brush off the warmness of his hand on me. His driving loses its smoothness.

'I have a feeling that you're not being honest with me, that you're hiding something.'

'I'm here to help you find Jack, that's all. Can't you believe me?'

'I guess the fact that my own mother and father have deceived me all my life and that my husband is a lying little shit doesn't predispose me to believe anyone that's all.'

'You don't have to tell me that there have been a lot of dishonest people in your life, but with you, at this very moment, and since I met you this morning, I have been truthful.'

'So you're not hiding anything? You have been totally straight with me?'

'No, I'm not saying that, exactly.'

'What are you saying, exactly?'

'I'm not going to lie to you, but there are things I know about that you don't need to know right now.'

'What the hell are you talking about, Frank?'

No response. He speeds up and takes a corner badly.

This line of conversation has upset him. I order him to pull over. I am going to flush him out before he kills us both in the process.

He stops at a small clearing that is the way into a farm gate. I get out of the car and walk around to his side and open the door. I ask him to get out. I get into the driver's seat and let the window down. I need a physical barrier between us. I have my hand on the ignition keys, ready to take off at any moment.

I know I should be careful about what I say to him. I know I should proceed slowly and try and think things through before I spurt them out, but my ability to reason is beginning to leave me.

The fear of never seeing Jack alive again is taking over. I take the drawing out of his coat pocket.

'What's this then? Why are you hiding it?'

Frank's face changes and the colour drains out of it. One of his hands covers his mouth.

'Oh sweet Jesus, you're right, I fucked up. I saw the drawing while Tommy was doing it. You were upstairs having a shower, remember? I realized I was wrong to let Derek go. I panicked. I didn't want you to know because I felt like such a bloody eejit. I thought I had lost the only connection we had to the kidnapper.'

'And we have, haven't we?'

'No, we haven't. Fortunately for us Tommy seems to have some sort of photographic memory. Did you notice how he put the numbers in on the plates? They are not complete but they are near to it. The guards obviously never asked him if he could recall the registrations.'

'Even if they had he wouldn't have been able to tell them. Tommy is all visual. He's totally dyslexic. He learns in pictures. So, what about it? How can we trace the registration?'

'The number plate on the bike that was at the cottage is a near match to one of these. See?' And he points to the black bike. 'I have a nephew in the guards at Store Street. He's doing a search on the PULSE system for me tonight when his shift starts. No questions asked.'

'You should have told me. How can I trust you now when I know you have been hiding something from me?'

'I'm sorry, Helen. Please try and understand I just want Jack to be safe; that is my only priority here.'

'Why? What's he to you? You've never even met him.'

'That's true, I have never met him.'

'Remember back at my house when the guards were there and you saw the photograph of Jack? You acted like you recognized him.'

'I swear, Helen, I never saw Jack before in my life.'

The words Frank are saying make logical sense but on another level they don't ring true. I know he is holding onto another piece of information. I can see anxiousness in him for the first time. His hand repeatedly goes through his hair. Funny, but Jack does that too when he's nervous. He holds on to the car window. His boots scrape the stony earth and his gaze avoids me.

'There's something you're not telling me, isn't there?'

He holds my arm firmly and stares at me directly.

'It's not a matter that we need to discuss now. It's of absolutely no relevance to finding Jack. Let's get going; we're losing time.'

I consider driving on by myself but decide against it. I let him back in and I drive. We make no attempt at talking. The car head-lights pick up the cats eyes on the black road and after a while it becomes monotonous.

Frank is taking up room in my thoughts. I am trying desperately to remember more about that summer long ago on the estate. The memories of the parties are hazy and time has put too much distance for me to recall the details lucidly. I desperately want to know what he knows and isn't telling me.

I can't wait to get back to Cillindara and grill my mother about Edgar and the will and my goddamn inheritance, the one she told me I never had, so that I can find out who took Jack and why. I hope that she is coherent enough to make sense.

At around two o'clock in the morning we arrive at the village of Cillindara. The tension between me and Frank is not resolved, but we talk enough to decide against stopping at Hill Street and go straight to the main house.

When we get there the gates to the front driveway are closed. That is not usual. There is an eerie stillness to the night. Frank pushes at the rusty black iron gates and they jerk open unsteadily. He climbs back into the car. I am nervous.

I drive slowly, creeping along. The noise that the tyres make on the driveway gravel is deafening. The moon is half obscured by thin, foggy clouds. Wisteria covers the front of the house; its shadows land on us as we get out of the car. We stand, speckled, on the front porch way. The house is in darkness except for the flicker of a candle I can see in the front room.

I climb the granite steps and ring the doorbell. There is no sound of it from the outside. I wait for long moments and can hear no noise of approaching footsteps.

'Maybe Charlie is round the back in his own house,' I suggest in a whisper.

We wait some more, at first, patiently and gradually with irritation. I had expected answers, I had expected Karl at least would have made it by now. I bang on the door with more urgency. There is still no reply.

We decide to go and look around the back when I hear a shuffling on the other side of the front door.

'Is that you, Charlie?' comes a elderly voice.

'No, it's me, Helen Raff … Helen Royston.'

The hall door opens and after a moment I recognize Mrs Molloy standing in the moonlight. She makes no attempt to illuminate the night any further. She is wearing a dressing-gown and we have obviously woken her up. I didn't know she stayed here anymore. Charlie had told me that she had retired and only came back once a week to do a few hours. It was a courtesy on my mother's part, to supplement her pension. Something is not right. As she asks us in I can see that she has been crying. There is a handkerchief in her hand and she keeps wringing it between her fingers.

'You're too late, miss, she's gone: your mother's dead.'

22

The Associates

I KEEP LOOKING AT Mrs Molloy and hoping that what she has just said is somehow going to be undone. I can't take this in. I am aware of Frank standing beside me and putting his arm around my shoulder. I lean into him, afraid that I will fall.

This is happening, her death is real, I keep telling myself but the defined lines of reality are getting hazy and imprecise. *No, this is not the waking world. I am dreaming. I am still asleep in the bedroom upstairs, the one with the roses on the wallpaper, and none of this is happening. Jack is safe at home and my mother is still alive.* I want to believe this so much.

'I'm sorry, Helen, I'm so sorry,' Frank is saying.

I turn and look at him and, as I do, every single movement that I make, is purposeful, exaggerated. I become aware of my breathing and as I exhale I sink further into him, checking that he is actually here. Yes, he is here and I am fully awake.

'It was very peaceful in the end, she went very softly like,' Mrs Molloy says.

Softly? Peaceful? As I stand myself up straight I know those words don't describe my mother to me. When I think of her I see the space inbetween her eyebrows forming into a frown. She mostly frowned; her mood with me was often dark and angry. After a few moments I begin to get angry too. How could she die now? It is almost as if this is her final act of defiance against me. She chose to die when there are so many fragments of my past that I don't understand. I had needed so much to talk to her, to ask her to fill in the missing details about Donntra, Ballytain, Edgar, me. I had wanted to tell her that I understood now, that with all I had found out over the last twenty-four hours I had begun to see her differently. Subconsciously I had pictured another visit with her when this was all over; a visit that would end in forgiveness and reconciliation. Now she has gone and died on me as if to intentionally continue the mystery of her life in her death.

'She was asking for you right up till the end, and your boy, miss,' says Mrs Molloy.

She starts talking about the undertaker but I don't hear her properly. I can see her saying words but my brain isn't taking them in. Frank squeezes my arm as if to force me back to some clarity.

'That's why I'm here. I dressed her like. I put her in the clothes she chose. You can come in yourself, into the dining-room, and see.'

'What? You want me to see her clothes?'

'No, miss, I'm talking about her body. Charlie arranged for her to be carried down here after she passed over. She's in the dining-room, pet. We couldn't have people tramping up to the summer-house for the viewing.'

'The viewing?'

'The viewing of the body, miss. It's to take place tomorrow, in the afternoon, before she goes to the church. That's what she wanted. She was very exact in all the details, the priest, the prayers, the choir, it's all arranged. We're expecting a big crowd. Come in, miss. Come in out of the porch. And you, Mr Callan, isn't it? Come in and have a cup of something before you see her. You look beat out.'

I walk into the hall, following her, I try not to glance at the dining-room as we pass it but some instinct forces me to look. I have to see her now so that I can truly know that she is dead. The conflict with her is coming to an end. It's over. I look at Frank and he nods at me; he knows again what I am thinking. He takes my arm and leads me slowly into the dining-room. Mrs Molloy turns on the light for us.

I know the coffin is in the centre of the room but I take a while to look at it. I don't know if I can face it immediately. Instead I focus on the room itself which is at the back of the house overlooking the formal gardens. I can remember the box hedging and the smell of old roses but, as it's still black outside, the four large Georgian sash windows now only reflect the electric light. The walls have textured red wallpaper and the embossed parts of the pattern shine. The gilt mirror glistens over the marble fireplace. The brightness is incongruous, irreverent.

'Mrs Molloy, I think she'd like the curtains closed.'

She obliges and, blessing herself as she passes the coffin, she pulls over the heavy, burgundy-coloured, velvet drapes.

Normally, the big mahogany dining-table is in the middle of the room but now it has been moved over to the side under one of the windows. Odd to see it there not set with the best silverware and Waterford crystal. It instantly reminds me of the dinners I had to endure here with her that summer long ago. If she and Edgar were in for the evening they would more often than not have guests. I would be paraded out as if we were the perfect little family; the pretty presentable daughter returned from boarding-school in England. The guests would always ask the same question;

'And what are you planning to read at college, Helen?' as if my entire being could be defined by a chosen career path. 'Art college? How charmingly bohemian.' I can still hear my mother click her tongue in disapproval.

I hated those dinners when the guests were adults but when they arrived with their teenaged children it was even worse. Prissy Protestant girls who spent all their time riding horses or 'suitable' boys dressed in sports jackets and ties. I was supposed to befriend them as if, because we were of similar ages, we would automatically have something in common. Mother wanted me to be in with the 'right set' as she put it. In my defiance of her, I never obliged. But did I not comply in the end, Mother?

Frank firms his grip on my arm and I look away from the dining-table and around the rest of the room.

The oak floor is covered with a Turkish patterned rug. In the middle of the room there is a trestle table and on it stands the coffin. It's in dark wood too with brass handles. I imagine that she ordered it so that it would match the other furniture in the room. She was so meticulous in every detail, even to the end. I turn the dimmer switch down to its lowest setting and the chandelier exudes a dull, musty yellow light. Cautiously I make my way to the centre of the room. My pace is slow, a mixture of reverence and stealth. As I near the coffin I am almost creeping. Gradually her face comes into view. Of course it's a deathly white, but it's not scary like she was in real life. Mrs Molloy was correct; there's peacefulness to it. I stand over her, taking all of her in. She's wearing one of her Chanel suits, the blue one, which I'm sure was her favourite. She has matching blue crystal studs in her ears. Her hands are folded in prayer. I notice the faded liver spots over paper-thin, wrinkly skin, her baby-pink nail polish and the bands of whiteness on her fingers where her rings used to be. The lines on her forehead have relaxed and some of her youthful prettiness has returned. Still, the dead never look like the living and I am assured; Mother is gone.

I think of the photograph that we found in the cottage. I rummage around in my handbag and when I find it I place it in-between her thumbs and forefingers. She is stiff. I lean down and touch her face, I kiss her cheek. The coldness of her corpse, the unresponsiveness of her skin, the indescribable smell of nothing that is death, all combine to overwhelm me and quite suddenly I start to cry in loud sobs. It's the sort of crying I never do. I keep thinking of what might have been, if she had been able to tell me the truth about my father, if she had not been so repulsed by my first pregnancy, if that had not created such a huge rift between us, if only things had been different. Instead she is lying here alone in all the splendour that she strove so hard to keep. Was it worth it, Mother I want to ask her?

After a few minutes Frank leads me away and we go through the double doors to the drawing-room. He gets me a large drink of whiskey from the decanter and we continue on until we get to the conservatory. It's far enough away from her body. I take another of his cigarettes. He disappears and I hear him mumbling in soft tones to Mrs Molloy. I stop crying and try to stay clearheaded. I am extremely tired. The day has drained me so much emotionally that I can hardly function enough to use my limbs. I must think about Jack and what position my mother's death has put me in. The missing will still has to be found. Jack has to be all right. I have to go on.

'It's odd,' Frank says, as he joins me again in the conservatory. 'Mrs Molloy doesn't know where Charlie is. He drove back into town with the undertaker at about ten o'clock this evening and he hasn't been seen or heard of since.'

'What about Jack? Has she seen him?'

'No, she has no knowledge of him being here. Now where could Charlie have got to?'

'Is he not just in his own house around the back?'

'I don't know. I can't imagine that he would have fallen asleep with all this going on. He would have heard us pull up in the driveway. I'm going to have to drive into town and ask around. We need him to help us go through your mother's documents. He might be able to help us find the will.'

'The will? Surely it's more important that he tell us where Jack is. Forget the goddamn will.'

'Helen, I know that, but this matter will not be resolved until that document is found. I am sure of it.'

Why is he sure of it I wonder? Is it in his interest to find the will also?

'OK, I'll go and search my mother's study while you're gone to find Charlie. I can't believe that she wouldn't have kept some record of it. She was so very exact.'

I take a small sip of the whiskey and hand the nearly full glass back to Frank.

'Have you my phone, by the way?' he asks. 'My nephew, the guard, Kevin, he was on duty tonight. He was supposed to text me if he found anything on those bikes.'

I fish it out of my pocket and give it to him not before noticing that there are two messages on it.

'Well, what does it say?'

'It says the bike is registered in the name of a company called Prodigal Holdings. Does the name mean anything to you?'

'No. Nothing. You?'

Frank trawls his hand through his hair again and looks nervous, almost guilty.

'I have heard of it before, but I can't be sure in what context. I come across a lot of businesses in my line of work. It might come to me. If not, I can ring my PA in a couple of hours' time. She gets in early. She can do a search on the directors for me.'

'Is that all the message said? There's no other message?'

'No, not from Kevin.'

Frank is obvious in his evasiveness. I don't believe him. There were two messages on his phone. Why has he not mentioned the other one?

'You know something, don't you, Frank? Something you're not telling me.'

'I need to get to Charlie. I have my suspicions, that's all.'

'What suspicions? Don't you think its time you shared them with me? Jack is my son, he's my life.'

'Helen, there's no time now. Please, let's look for the will and try and get to Jack before … before it's too late.'

This is the first time Frank has admitted that Jack is in real danger. He scares me. Nevertheless his secrecy astounds me. How could he hold anything back from me now?

He goes to leave the conservatory but turns back when I call after him, 'I wish you would tell me whatever it is you know. Don't betray me, Frank, or I will come after you.'

'You don't have to threaten me, Helen. You can trust me, believe me. Your mother's death will bring this all to a head. We have to stay focused on finding this document. It's our only bargaining tool. You know that, don't you?'

I breathe, a deep purposeful breath before I speak.

'All I know is that I'm going to do everything in my power to get Jack back and that includes killing anyone who stands in my way.'

I surprise myself and him at the cold determination of my retort. I mean it. He stands awkwardly for a few seconds before he goes. My anger stays with me. I trust no one. Am I just a pawn in this intricate game of chess? How has the will surpassed the importance of my son's life?

'I want to get Jack back just as much as you do, Helen.'

'Go on then; find Charlie and call me if anything comes to light.'

After a few more moments I go back to the hall, avoiding the dining-room, and can hear Mrs Molloy still up in the kitchen. She is setting things out for tomorrow. The sound of clanging china cups and the polishing of teaspoons meets me as I descend the kitchen stairs.

'Go to bed now, Mrs Molloy. We can get some extra help in the morning for you.'

She agrees, reluctantly, and says she will just finish the last lot of drying. I make my way back up the stairs and on into my mother's office. This time I have no intention of politely searching the room. I grab a piece of paper and a pen and write down some headings.

Leads:
Hayes Cunningham
Why was there a break-in at his office?
Was someone searching for the will there?
Prodigal
Who owns this company and what dealings have they had with my mother?
Is Frank involved in this?
Karl's gallery insurance claims
How long has Karl been dealing with my mother?
Which one of them/were they both dishonest?
Charlie
Who was with him when I made the last call to him?
What else does he know?

First I approach her desk. The green leather top is clear except for a few pens and headed estate notepaper. There are drawers on the left-hand side. As I open them I see that the first two are mostly filled with office paraphernalia. Neat rows for paper clips, staples, file tags, markers, rubber bands, clear plastic change bags. There is nothing of any interest except a few photo albums in the bottom drawer. Another time I could leaf through them but not now. I fail to see their relevance.

There is a wooden filing cabinet to the side of the desk. I check the drawers there but they are locked. I look around the desk again for the key and begin pulling things askew in the desk drawers. When I am sure that there is no key I decide to try and lever the filing cabinet open. I scan the room for some sort of heavy implement. A set a fire irons catches my eye and I start to assess the effectiveness of prising the cabinet open with a poker. I awkwardly rush to fetch it and, as I do so, I knock into the open bottom drawer of the desk and some of the photos fall out of the albums. With the poker I begin to prise the cabinet open and after a few moments a loud cracking sound signals my success.

The files are incredibly neat and ordered. I scan the file tag names quickly: *staff wages, bank accounts, house insurance, art courses, estate tax returns*. The cabinet is packed tightly with them. It is going to take me a long time to sort through all of these. I concentrate on the financials utterly convinced now that Jack's disappearance has to do with money.

I check the bank file first and quickly review her current statements. It looks healthy enough with a current balance of nearly €7000. There doesn't seem to be any outstanding loans or overdrafts. The statements go back for a long number of years, even before Edgar died. The financial history looks radically different then. I notice that before he died the accounts were constantly overdrawn. Letters of warning from the bank intersperse the statements:

Dear Mr Royston
We can no longer continue to give you an extended line of credit ...

is the general gist of them. The debt and negative balances continue on after his death until 1993. After that the financial picture changes radically. All loans are paid off with one big lump sum of £(IR)150,000 being deposited. That was a considerable sum then. It is over €200,000 in today's money. I try and think where the money could have come from. Did she sell a painting perhaps? Then there seems to be a pattern of lump sums deposited into her accounts – irregular payments of at least a couple of grand at a time. There is a large payment of £(IR)125,000 and another of £(IR)20,000 but no record of what they were for. What was she trading in?

I chide myself for not taking more notice of her art collection. I know that the Royston art collection is valuable. At least one Jack B. Yeats, a le Broquy, a bequest from Derek Hill ... what else, Helen, think of what else? I think of checking the house to see if the paintings are still *in situ* but I am afraid of going into the dining-room now on my own and being close to her body. My fear of her is still very much alive in me even though she is dead.

The notion of forgery comes to mind. Even if I checked out the paintings I wouldn't be able to tell if they were genuine or not. Was she selling off the family collection to get herself out of financial trouble and substituting the paintings with forgeries that Karl had provided? That would make sense, but what is the connection? What has this got to do with Jack being taken? Did they sell a forgery and were they found out? Is this why Karl is being charged?

I recall the wording of the ransom note – *find your father's will* – so even if she was dealing in art with Karl and selling off the Royston collection to keep her going what would that have to do with my father's will?

I think back over the events of the day, my mind racing trying to order the information.

I jot down a few more notes.

Blackmail by Karl: But what was the reason? ... what did he have on her?
Selling of the family art collection using Karl as a legitimate dealer?
Being involved in forgery with Karl?

They seem to me to be the only possibilities.

I am lost in thought when Mrs Molloy's head appears around the office door. She is on her way to bed. She startles me.

'Is there anything at all I can do for you, miss?' she says, eyeing the forced-open filing cabinet.

I try to recover my composure.

'Ah Mrs Molloy. Don't worry about the cabinet. I needed to find some documents urgently that's all.'

She reddens and looks nervous.

I feel a bit of my father coming on, a bit of Royston in me.

'Mrs Molloy. I'm in charge now. My mother would have wanted it this way.'

I am not sure at all about the truth of that statement, but Mrs Molloy needs reassurance. It doesn't exactly look good, me rifling through filing cabinets when my mother is hardly cold in the dining-room.

'Is there anything I can help you with?'

'Thank you, Mrs Molloy, and indeed you could help by telling me who was here in the last couple of weeks.'

'She did have a lot of visitors. We all knew she was ... she was ...'

'Dying? Mrs Molloy?'

'Yes.'

'So who was here? It's very important that you remember everyone.'

'Well there were her ladies from the book club, and then the Friends of the National Gallery. She knew quite a few people in that group. They had lovely parties here. It was only last summer when she had the marquee up in the garden. A hundred and fifty people, and all to be catered for. You should have seen—'

'Please, Mrs Molloy, just try and stick to the last couple of weeks.'

'Sorry, miss. There was the vicar, Oliver Pomfrey, he came often, but do you know that in the end she asked for the Catholic priest? As far as I know she hadn't been to a Catholic church for years, but Father O'Donnell gave her the last rites just before she went.'

'I'd say that was a great comfort to her, Mrs Molloy.' I remember mother had changed religion when she married Edgar. How strange that was for an Irish Catholic country girl to abandon her own faith. Was it connected to with the way she was treated in her own home place when I came along out of wedlock? Had she been disillusioned then? Religion had been another issue of conflict between us. She had wanted me to become a member of the Church of Ireland when I had finished school. I had refused. Edgar wasn't fussed so in the end the matter was dropped. Nevertheless she attended local services with Edgar for most of her married life. Was it a testament to the double life she led that she turned back to the faith of her birth when death was upon her? But I am allowing myself to get distracted. I concentrate again on Mrs Molloy.

'But anyone else. Her solicitor? An accountant perhaps?'

'No, no one like that. Not that I can recall. But you know, miss, I'm not here all the time now like I used be. But, goodness gracious, I'm leaving out her gentlemen business partners.'

'And they were?'

'Mr Callan and Mr Grainger, of course.'

'Oh!' I say, trying to hide the look of shock from my face.

'What business would they have had together, Mrs Molloy?' I ask, as I feel my heartbeat quicken and the nausea coming back.

'I wouldn't really know the details, but those gentlemen are in the property, aren't they? It could have been something to do with sites on the land like. I don't know, it was never discussed with me. I'm only the housekeeper, miss.'

'I'm sorry to be pressing you like this, Mrs Molloy. It's very important. What do you know about the sites on the land?'

'Oh, just the usual, miss, that they were applying for planning. You know the big road is coming through here, don't you? And that if they can change it from agricultural to residential it will make the land a lot more valuable? Sure the whole town knows that.'

'No, I didn't know.' I reproach myself for my own stupidity. 'And Mr Callan and Mr Grainger were helping her with the change of zoning?'

'Yes, I think so, something like that.'

'If you remember anything else, you come and tell me straight-away. Will you promise me that you will do that?'

'Yes, of course, I will, miss.'

I expect her to leave the room but she stands awkwardly at the door.

'Do you know how much she talked about you? How proud she was of you, the way you are bringing up your boy.'

That is an odd a remark to make.

'But she hardly saw him; she never came to visit.'

'Oh, she knew what was going on.'

'What … what are you talking about?'

'Your Mr Rafferty would be here with the photographs.'

'Mr Rafferty? My husband Karl?'

'Yes, I presumed you would have known. That's why I didn't mention him before.'

I try desperately to hide my surprise but notice a sternness creep into my tone.

'What photographs?'

'He'd be here on and off over the years. They had business together.'

I try to stay outwardly calm, but inside I realize the significance of this remark.

'What business would that have been, Mrs Molloy?'

'To do with the pictures.'

I look at her blankly.

'Pictures or photographs, Mrs Molly? Please be clear.'

'The art pictures was their business.'

'Oh, you mean the paintings.'

'Yes. He would come down with new ones sometimes and at other times he would take some away.'

'Oh, I see. I didn't know that. And the photographs?'

'At the end of their business they'd sit in the conservatory, over drinks, and Mr Rafferty would produce a new batch of photographs for her. They'd be all of your young lad, Jack, isn't it? She'd be never finished going through them.'

'Is that so?'

So Karl was trading with my mother all these years and I never knew about it. The connection should have been obvious. After my father died she did a fine art appreciation course in Dublin. I was vaguely aware of her beginning to deal in Irish art and at first, way before Jack was born, she would ask me to openings of exhibitions in Dublin. She felt that she had finally got to mix 'in the right circles' as she called it and wanted me to be part of it all. Occasionally I would turn up, gulp down free wine and make my excuses before she started introducing me to anyone. Once I got drunk and embarrassed her and that was the end of the invites. I wonder did Karl know her before he met me? Would he have realized I was her daughter? Is that how she knew Karl was in gaol? Her business relationship with Karl is hard enough to fathom, but for her to take an interest in my Jack is astounding. I had longed for him to have a doting granny. She could have asked me directly to see him. Why all the secrecy between the two of them? Why had I not known about this?

My memory goes back to when Karl was in gaol. Jack was born and I had dropped out of college as I just couldn't manage to support us and study at the same time. I had a job in the mornings in an architect's office, but they let me go when I kept missing time when Jack was ill. I couldn't bear to leave him even if he had the slightest snuffle. I tried doing typing work at home but it had been too sporadic to rely on. Finally I had applied for the unmarried mother's allowance and was just about scraping by when he was released.

Our finances changed quite dramatically then. He claimed he

had been left the property in Molesworth Street by his godfather, an uncle with no children of his own. I was so relieved that Karl could now have a premises for his art deals. It legitimized him. I never questioned the validity of the bequest. I had been introduced to Karl's parents once. They were surprisingly ordinary conservative people, not at all what I would have expected. Contact had more or less ceased with them when he got a custodial sentence. They had retired to Spain just after we were married and Karl had never liked it when I had suggested meeting them. Was the bequest real, or had it something to do with my mother?

His gallery had done decidedly well for what is a precarious start up business. For years I was baffled when he came up so readily with cash, that he didn't fritter away all the profits. Could he have been blackmailing my mother? Is that the connection between them and Jack's kidnapping?

The business side of it is odd enough but now that I know she had photographs of Jack as well I wonder has it got any relevance? Did someone get hold of those photos of Jack and use them to set up his abduction? He was taken from me, but has his kidnapping more to do with her?

'Sometimes they didn't get on you know,' Mrs Molloy continues in a hushed voice disturbing me from my reflections.

'Oh they didn't? In what way?'

'I used to hear them fighting. Usually over money. I thought that was the reason you and her, you know, weren't close.'

'No, Mrs Molloy, that wasn't it. I never even knew Karl was here. Can you believe that? There's a lot going on here that I have been ignorant of. Who else came here in the last couple of weeks? Did anyone come and talk to her? Did she give the photographs to anyone?'

'No, not that I know of. But the strange thing is she kept all those photographs, I'm sure of it, but for the life of me I don't know where they are in the house.'

'I'm sure I will come across them. Now off you go to bed. There is a big day ahead of us tomorrow.'

Mrs Molloy smiles and fades away out the door as silently as she entered.

Frank must have been in on this all along. He told me he had fallen out with Nick Grainger, but that can't be true if he was still coming down here with him. Of course, the estate would be worth a fortune if it could be used as development land. Wasn't it staring me in the face? Why had I not thought about it?

I am pondering my conversation with Mrs Molloy when the phone rings and makes me jump with nervousness. The last time I answered this phone was when Karl told me Jack was missing.

I am fearful of more bad news and answer hesitantly.

'Helen, it's me, Frank.'

'Christ, Frank, where are you? Have you found out anything else?'

'I'm at your old house at Hill Street. I think you'd better get down here.'

'Why? Is Jack there? Please tell me he's there.'

'I'm sorry, Helen, he isn't, but you need to get down here straight away.'

'Right now I'm going through my mother's files. There are lots of surprising revelations here. Unless you can give me a good reason to get down there I am staying put.'

'Her files? Be careful, Helen, you might find something in there that you don't need to know just yet.'

The effrontery of this last statement really gets my heckles up.

'Who the hell do you think you are, telling me what I need to know? You completely failed to mention throughout the entire time I have been with you that Nicholas Grainger and yourself have business dealings with my mother. It's about time you came clean and told me exactly what your interest is in this affair. I think you are directly involved in Jack's disappearance and that you have been leading me along all day with your false concern.' I hadn't meant that all to come out but there is no time to mask my fears.

There is momentary silence at the other end.

'Helen you have to understand that there is no way in the world

I had anything to do with Jack being taken and that I would never ever harm him. But you're right, you're perfectly right, I should have told you from the beginning. I thought I could avoid it, that I could sort this all out, but now I know I was wrong. Come down here and I will explain everything. I'm sorry, Helen. Please get down here as fast as you can.'

'How do I know this is not part of your plan? I think I should call Detective O'Meara right now and have you arrested.'

'I know this is a huge leap of faith for you but the guards will only put Jack in more danger. Please get here quickly.'

'Not until you tell me why. What's going on down there?'

'Karl's here for a start. But there's something else you should see. It might help you understand what's going on. Honestly, I didn't understand it all myself. Come right away.'

Silence again as I consider my options. What choice do I have?

'But how, Frank? How am I going to get there? You've taken the rental car.'

Then I remember that my own car is here. I drove down last night and parked around the side of the house. I upturn the contents of my bag and realize that in my panic I have left the keys at home in my house in Dublin.

'I'm stuck here with no keys to my car.'

'Your mother's car is in the garage. The keys are always kept above the Aga in the kitchen. Come as soon as you can.'

'But how…?'

Click. The phone has gone dead. How did Frank know about the keys? He must be extremely familiar with Cillindara House to have that information. What the hell is going on here?

I need to get to the house in Hill Street and confront Frank with this. I suspect that Nicholas was involved in taking Jack and that it had something to do with forged paintings or a land deal. Just how much Frank knows and if he was part of the plan is what I have to establish. I shunt the filing cabinet drawer closed and then I notice that the bottom drawer of the desk, the one where the photo albums have fallen out, is still open. I go to close it and start putting the photos back into the album in a haphazard fashion even though I know it is not important and I could do it later. Hysteria is abated momentarily by the banal. As I stuff the last photo into the back cover I recognize someone in it before it is fully out of sight. I take it out again and examine it closely.

It's of my mother, years ago; about the time I was at university in Dublin. It is not her that has caught my eye though, it's the man with her. He has his arm around her waist, territorially, as if they are a couple. He's looking into her eyes and smiling adoringly. I stare at his face in disbelief. He's younger, but he looks just as he did when I first met him.

It's Karl.

23

The Photograph

I STARE AT THE photo at first not quite understanding what I am seeing. The words that Karl spoke to me a few hours ago come back to me verbatim: '*I knew your mother before I met you. I should have told you a long time ago.*' Is that what he meant? Was he *with* her? Jesus, the thought of Karl and my mother is inconceivable. It is repulsive. I sit heavily into the desk chair.

As I look at the photograph, amid my bitterness and anger, it makes sense. That bastard! Did he ever look at me like that? I think of him with my mother and utter betrayal pervades my being. How could he have been my husband and have been with her, my mother, my nemesis? I relive everything I told Karl about her, my fractured upbringing, the way she distanced herself from me when she married Edgar, the terrible loss I felt when Edgar, whom I now know to be my true father, had died. I had opened my soul up to him, there for the taking, and all the time he had known. He must have known everything about me from her as well as from me. That fucking bastard, is all I can think and repeat aloud, 'that fucking bastard'. I want to scream abuse at him; I want to hit him hard until it hurts him. I rummage through the rest of the album, searching for more evidence, hoping that I am wrong. I start to think about their ages. Karl was thirty-eight when I met him and it looks like my mother knew him around about that time. When I left college she would have been in her late-forties. That would make her only about eight to ten years older than him. It is imminently possible then that they did indeed have an affair. How long did it go on for though and what has it got to do with Jack being missing?

There are more photos of the two of them but none with that subtle look that portrays them as a couple. The pictures seem to have been taken at an art gallery, with lots of Dublin society types about. There is one of my mother standing beside a painting. It's a Sean Keating. I'm sure the same one is hanging in the drawing-room. Perhaps he advised her on pieces to purchase. That, I can understand, but why did he carry on an open affair with me when he had been with her? Who did it benefit, or more importantly, who did it hurt? What is he doing at Hill Street anyway? An image of his face comes into my head. I am getting uncontrollably angry.

My mother's resentful attitude towards me is now becoming all so painfully clear. First, I was the child out of wedlock, the one responsible for her being ostracized from her own village and losing her job. Then, when I became pregnant as a teenager she must have thought that I would repeat the pattern she had set. Finally I ended up with her lover. I never knew that our lives were so intertwined, that we were so close.

She had always given the impression that she could not abide Karl. I had tried to hide the fact that he was in gaol from her but, of course, in the way that all mothers do, she had found out in the end. '*Shacked up with a man with a prison record – I wouldn't have expected anything else.*' I remember her practically spitting at me at one of our infrequent meetings. I never did know how she knew about his gaol sentence.

I kick the bottom drawer closed and start flinging the photographs around the room. I pick up the poker and start lashing it against the fireplace in an attempt to vent some of my anger. Oh I can blame him, I can blame her, but most of all I can blame myself. How could I have lived this life of being led along, as if I had no choice in my own path, as if I was a minor actor in someone else's script? Whatever I think about them it's me who did this. I went along blindly with other people's plans. First my mother's, then

Karl's and now Frank and Nick's. I am damned sure I will not continue to play this ridiculous charade.

I keep bashing the poker on the fireplace and the noise I am making momentarily shuts out another sound coming from the driveway. There's a car pulling up. I switch off the study light and peer through the front window.

It's the guards. I recognize Detectives Malone and O'Meara approaching the front door. I have to think quickly. This is impossible. Is it worth trying to fill them in on all of this, or would it just take too long to explain? I could risk being arrested. What is it going to sound like when I tell him we were all lying to them in my house this morning, that I don't know where Jack is: I think Frank is involved in Jack's disappearance and that my husband has probably contributed to the situation by being involved in fraudulent art dealings? No, there is no way that Detective Malone will be sympathetic and it could endanger Jack further by introducing more delays.

Jack, how am I going to get you back safe and unharmed when I still can't work out the motive for your disappearance?

I decide to make a run for it and take the bank file with me. I need answers and if I can confront Frank and Karl with the statements they will have to explain.

I race down the kitchen stairs and grab my mother's car keys. The detectives are already knocking on the front door. As I exit through the basement door I can hear the knocking get louder and more frequent.

I run out to the stable yard and hope to Christ the old hay shed, which is now used as a garage, is not locked. Thankfully there is no padlock on the rusting sliding catch and I quietly open the large wooden doors. I think I can hear the detectives walking around the outside of the house and wonder how badly it would look if I was caught making an escape. I look at her old silver-grey Mercedes. Maybe it has been garaged for a long time. Will it start immediately? I fear the noise of the engine will give me away before I make it to the front door. The village is nearly two miles away and, if they gave chase in their car, they would probably catch up with me. I hide for a few moments behind the door and think what best to do. Making my way to the back of the garage I stumble over an old bicycle. OK this is it then, I decide, this is my safest way out of here.

I secure the bank file carefully to the back carrier and, as noiselessly as I can, I begin to push the bike towards the old oak tree at the side of the house. I hide in the shadow of branches for a few moments. I have a clear view of the front door.

'Have you no respect for the dead,' I catch Mrs Molloy saying and hear some mumbled words by the detectives before I see them enter the house.

This is it, my only chance; I mount the bike and pedal furiously down the front driveway. I can feel the blood pumping and pulsating around my head. I keep looking over my shoulder to see if they have been alerted to the noise of the bike and are following me.

Keep it together, Helen, I keep telling myself. You are going to get Jack back. This day will end and all will be resolved.

I take a sharp right and head towards the village.

24

The Past

THE COLD NIGHT AIR rushes past my face and I am refreshed. I wonder why I rarely feel the day. I am alive. I pedal faster and faster still not sure if I am being chased. I think about the labyrinth of deception that surrounds me. The puzzle is beginning to unravel.

My father's will must declare me as the true heir to the estate. That is the only explanation for what is going on here. Why could she never tell me who he really was? I can understand that she may have kept it from me when I was a child, but what was the use in concealing my parentage as an adult? Whatever her reasons were, her actions have now put Jack's life at risk. The bitch. The fucking bitch. I am glad that she is dead. Rotting in her own pomposity.

But what about Frank Callan and Nick Grainger? From what I have learned their business affairs with her were extensive. Frank himself admitted to me earlier on that he had dealings with her. What were they exactly? Why would they have an interest in getting the estate lands re-zoned? Will the discovery of what Edgar left me help them in some way? What on earth is in that will?

I am troubled because the idea that Frank has been playing me all day does not fit with the character of the man I have been with for the last sixteen hours. He is successful in his own right and doesn't need more money. Then I remember what he said about Nicholas and it confuses me. He told me he didn't work with him anymore, implied he didn't like him or trust him. He was nervous when his name was mentioned. If Nicholas Grainger is involved in this, is Frank working with me or against me? I have a vague hope that Frank is telling the truth but I cannot be sure, I cannot trust anyone. I must get Jack. I must get Jack. I say it again and again in my head.

I reach the sleeping village and stop pedalling. In this light the townscape appears unchanged from when I was a child. I dismount the bike when I reach Hill Street. I try to lurk in the shadows of the eaves of the houses and slowly walk to the end of the terrace. Taking a left turn into the back lane I am sure that I am not followed. I notice the former grass and mud track has been replaced with gravel. The bike is dumped by throwing it down with a loud clatter. I should not be making noise and try to make up for it by softly treading the pebbled pathway. I want to surprise Frank by entering through the back.

The wooden garden gate is brown and rusty, exactly as I remember it. I try to open it silently but it makes a loud creak. I am plunged into darker shadow and realize that there have been mews buildings built in the gardens of the adjoining houses. Our garden is untouched. The same as it was in the seventies. The little vegetable patch is still cared for and tended to. The compost heap is still attracting midges in the mid-summer night. I can make out lettuce and cabbages in the fading moonlight. She was always fond of cabbage, my mother, a vegetable I have never been able to stomach since I was a child. I remember the smell of it boiling in the kitchen. It makes me want to retch.

I make my way down the mud path, through the opening in the hedge, passing the roses and the perfectly weeded flower beds. Who lives here now, I wonder? Why is it so well tended? Why has it not been changed?

I try the back door, remembering that we never locked it. For one second I am back to those long years ago when I came back from school and let myself into an empty house on my own, waiting for Mother to come home for tea. And here I am again after all those years, alone.

As my hand reaches for the metal latch I chastize myself for even thinking it would be still unlocked. To my surprise it is and it opens easily. There is no light on downstairs and I can hear no voices. Suddenly I am frightened, frightened of this lonely loveless house as I was as a child; afraid of the shadows and the strangers that they might hide; afraid of the unexplained noises and creaks of this mean little home.

I see there is a light on upstairs and I make my way past the Formica kitchen table. Oddly again there is no change and the furniture is the same as when I lived here with her. Through the dim light I can see that the table is set for two. Willow-patterned china cups and saucers, the matching milk jug and sugar bowl, the ebony handled knives and forks exactly positioned; it is as it was.

The eeriness of the house is in me now as it was then. I hear the grandfather clock ticking away in the hallway. I glimpse the raised floral patterned armchairs in the living-room. I feel as if I have intruded onto a stage of a theatre where the actors have long gone and played their part.

I slip my shoes off at the bottom of the stairs, a reflex reaction, not to disturb Mother in her sleep. 'Don't make a racket, you'll upset the neighbours with all your loud clumping around,' she would say. I take to the stairs slowly, remembering each step, avoiding the creaking risers. I get to the upstairs landing and see a light on in her room. The fear of her here is still with me now. She is dead, Helen, she is dead, I keep repeating to myself. You left her cold body in the dining-room of Cillindara House less than half an hour ago. But somehow I can feel her spirit here much stronger than it was in the cold formal dining-room of my father's house.

I creep towards her door. I see Karl sitting on her bed, on top of her pale-pink satin eiderdown, his body at ease in what should surely be an unfamiliar place for him. He has a glass of wine in one hand, a cigar in the other. I stare at him with utter contempt.

As I enter the room I know there is no one else about, no Frank, no Jack, and even though Karl is here, I am alone, again. A strange relief washes over me and mixes up with anxiousness and guilt. Am

I no further on to finding Jack? When will this puzzle come together? When will this nightmare end?

I go to speak to Karl but instead he directs me to the other side of the room. A glimpse of colour catches my eye. I notice that her old wardrobe doors are open. It's then that I see it and am completely surprised. Like a shrine the inside doors of the wardrobe are covered in photographs. They are put together like a mosaic, plastered over every square inch of the cheap laminate wood, even in the chaos of the mosaic there is a sort of chronological order. They are all photographs of Jack. They start when he was a baby, then Jack when he was a toddler, Jack at his first day at school, Jack in the Nativity play, Jack opening his Christmas presents, Jack blowing out his birthday candles, Jack on his first pair of rollerblades, Jack on his mountain bike, Jack on his skateboard. How did she get these? There is only one possible explanation: Karl must have supplied her with all of these. There is no other source. Over all these years he has been in contact with her then. All this time he was coming down to Cillindara, involved in whatever shady art dealings they had, and supplying her with details of my Jack. These are the photos that Mrs Molloy was talking about.

I feel violated, raped, my private life invaded. That she should take such a covert interest in Jack instead of just asking me directly if she could see him is bizarre. Why could she not have a normal relationship with her only grandson instead of all this subterfuge?

I turn my attention to Karl.

'You'd better tell me what's going on here right now.'

His response is slow and languid. He takes a pull of his cigar and then sips his wine. He is half drunk. I am well used to that. But how could he do this now when Jack's life is at stake?

'What is happening here, Karl? Where is Jack? What is your involvement in this? Tell me now, Karl, now.'

He starts to answer, with words that are so slurred it is difficult to understand him.

'Never knew ... you never knew.'

'I never knew what, Karl?'

'Photographs, all the photographs …'

'The ones on the wardrobe, is that what you're talking about?'

'He was the boy, the boy she never had for Edgar. Do you understand now?'

'My mother wanted to have another child, is that what you are saying?'

'Yes, but it never happened. Oh she got pregnant all right; many times, but she lost them, all of them.'

'You're saying that she was pregnant by Edgar and had miscarriages. What has that got to do with anything?'

'Didn't you ever wonder why Edgar married her? Why she hated you so much? She couldn't have another child for him. She blamed you, blamed you for everything, even for his affairs.'

My father having affairs is no real news to me. I long suspected it; I was aware of his ability to charm the opposite sex, but like the other distasteful parts on my past I had never consciously thought of it.

'What are you saying? For Christ's sake, can you sober up and talk some sense? Come into the bathroom and take some water.'

He agrees and I help him into the bathroom, his arm across my shoulder. I am supporting what seems like his full weight. My anger takes hold and rather than wait for him to sip water from the tap I push him into the bath and turn on the shower tap. I direct the weak flow of cold water onto his face. His clothes get wet in the process. He is annoyed but takes one look at me and decides that there is no point in protesting.

He turns to me, his eyes not quite focused, and says, 'Your father, Edgar, he wanted a son to replace the one who died in the hunting accident. What was his name – Julius?'

'No, it was Julian. He died at sixteen when he fell off his mount and the horse rolled over on him. I have told you all this already. What on earth has it got to do with Jack?'

'It's got everything to do with Jack. Don't you see that Edgar married her in the hope of having another son? When it didn't turn out like that for them she was heartbroken. Then when you got pregnant after Edgar died she was still so traumatized by all her miscarriages that she pretended … pretended Jack was hers, you see. That's why I had to bring her the photos. Every week, every two weeks. She said she would tell; tell you everything if I didn't.'

Jesus Christ Almighty, how screwed up is that? How many miscarriages did she have? Is that why I spent my summers away from the estate with Edgar? Is that what he meant when he said 'her nerves were at her'?

'Karl, get to the point. You knew all along that Edgar was my father, that I would inherit. Is that why you stayed with me all these years? Professing to be my husband so that you could come into some money? You're some bastard, Karl. What else?'

I start shaking him now, surprised at my own violence. He sits up in the bath. His eyes are red and bloodshot. If he wasn't drunk I would imagine that he had been crying.

'I tried to talk to you earlier, but you were too busy with Frank. Is he your new boyfriend, Helen?'

Boyfriend? Whatever gave him that impression? Yes it's true, I admit fleetingly to myself, I am attracted to Frank, but this is not the time to think of that.

'Don't be ridiculous. What on earth makes you say that?'

'He's rather territorial about you, didn't you notice?'

'Stick to the point, Karl. What did you want to tell me earlier? That you had an affair with my mother before you met me, was that it? Were you screwing her and me at the same time? Is that what you had to say to me?'

He slumps back in the bath and closes his eyes. He begins to laugh.

'You never worked it out, did you?'

'Worked out what?'

'The bust, the drugs bust. It was her. Didn't you ever wonder who dobbed me in? How the cops got the address? How did they know which morning to come? Any other day, any other fucking day, and there wouldn't have been enough to do me. I nearly got done with intent to supply.'

'What? Why? Were you and her over or ... or what?'

'We had split up at her behest. At first I fitted her requirements. I introduced her to all the society types and she liked my accent, my public-school education. I think I reminded her of Edgar, but ... but—'

'She saw through the mask, did she, Karl? She was quicker than me, wasn't she?'

I think about the years I believed in him, believed in the image that he had created: The consummate man about town; his good looks; his nice manners; his dapper dress sense. On his mantelpiece in Morehampton Road there would be a string of invitations to drinks parties, society weddings, gallery openings. He was so blasé too about the way he spent money; it all added to his appeal: bottles of Cristal in Lilly's; bouquets of roses for any minor occasion; an ounce of coke here and there; weekends in Paris; a box at Cheltenham. Once he even hired a helicopter to bring us to a U2 concert in Slane. He was everywhere in the eighties but even then I should have seen that he was all panache and no substance. That was all before, before he got sent away.

Karl slumps back in the bath now and almost smiles.

'No, there was no mask for her. She tired of me quickly. I was just a fling, a toy boy, a momentary indiscretion. I was nothing to her. But, oh she was sorry afterwards ... didn't know I would get sent down ... didn't know what she was letting herself in for.'

'What do you mean? Why would she have bothered with you, Karl? She had finished with you. You said so.'

'Oh my dear Helen, how naïve you still are. I knew you were her daughter and at first I went out with you to get back at her. She had insulted me, an older woman casting me aside. She found out of course. That was my intention. One of those Dublin Four bitches told her soon enough and she tried to split us up. That's what the bust was about. Don't you see?'

I remember that Garda now, the senior one standing in the bedroom on the morning of the bust. He told me to get dressed and to go home to my mother.

Karl has sobered up somewhat and is talking freely. I let him go with it.

'She wanted me out of the way, out of your life, but it didn't work out according to her plans. Yes but it was a different story then when she realized there would be a grandchild involved. She had to look after me then didn't she?'

'What are you talking about, Karl?'

'The bequest. You believed I had been left an entire building by a distant uncle? You've met my parents. They are not from money. Don't you see we did a deal? She put a deposit on the gallery for me and we started dealing in art together.'

'How on earth did she come up with the money for a deposit on a building on Molesworth Street?'

'I don't know. She must have sold something. She always had money your mother.'

No, I think, she didn't. How did she finance this? Was she in massive debt? Is that what the sale of Ballytain was about?

'What about the money for the deposit on the first house I bought and did up? Where did that come from? You told me you had got a great price on a painting. Was that true?'

'No, Helen, it wasn't. She provided it. Did you really believe I was making all that money myself?'

'You're telling me that my mother set me up in my first property transaction and I never knew? How could you have lied to me all this time?'

'I didn't mean for it to continue, I swear it, Helen, but once I started I couldn't stop. It was too complicated.'

'What business did you have with her? Was it forgeries? Were you dealing in forgeries with her? Is that it? Is that why Jack was taken?'

'Look, most of our business was legit. I can't connect any later shenanigans with Jack. She needed to raise as much cash as possible to pay someone off, that's what the insurance scam was about, but I don't know who it was. Neither do I know why Jack was taken, but I do know that he wasn't taken from you, he was taken from *her*.

Someone knew how much she idolized the boy and is using that now.'

'But she's dead, Karl. She's dead. How on earth are we going to find out now? Have you ever seen the will? What the hell is in it?'

'No one has ever seen that document except Edgar, your mother and that solicitor who's dead now. The fellow from Cork. The old man.'

'Lynch, yes, Lynch, but it must have been given to his son-in law, Hayes Cunningham. That must be why they broke into his office.'

'No, you don't understand. There was only ever one copy. Whoever broke into that solicitor's office didn't get anything. She kept the only copy herself. She told me that a long time ago. But she never told me where it was.'

Karl and I stare at each other now. I am looking at a man whom I thought was my husband. A man I trusted. A man I loved; a man I forgave so many times; a man who disappointed me so often, and now he has told me all this my world has truly crumbled. How could he? What right did he have to live off my mother like this? How could he have deceived me for so long?

'How could you do this, Karl? How could you do this to me and your only son Jack?'

He continues to stare at me, but now I can see a hint of pleading in his eyes; it's almost as if he is asking for forgiveness. He is about to speak again. Is it possible that he is actually going to apologize? What does it matter if he does? He has totally betrayed me.

The silence is broken when I hear a message tone on my phone. I run back into the bedroom and grab my mobile from my jacket. It's a message from Frank.

Meet me at the old entrance to the estate. The way we used to break in. Get out of Hill Street now. You are in danger. Get out.

I rush back into the bathroom and see that Karl's head is slumped between his knees and he has started to cry.

'I don't know how this is going to turn out, now that she is dead.

I don't know what's going to happen to Jack. I love him; I love him just as much as you.'

I have seen him like this before, weak and vulnerable. When he first got out of gaol I made allowances for him. Now that I know what he has done I will not soften.

'So that was it, was it, Karl? You married me because you could get money out of my mother, repair your reputation and stay with your son. Did I ever come into it at all?'

'Oh come now, Helen, you were young and lovely and I was very taken with you.'

'*Taken with me*? Is that all you can say after fifteen years? *Taken with me*? More likely you were taken with my mother's money. Forget about it now. You can be sure that any conversation I will be having with you in the future will be to do with the terms of our divorce. I have to get out of here. Stop crying and tell me quickly what else you know. Who are they?'

I hear a noise at the front door as if someone is letting themselves in. Panic sets in and I desperately try to work out what to do next.

'I've only met Nick, the one who posed as a client. I don't know who else is involved. That's all I know.'

I can hear the front door close and heavy fast footsteps in the hall.

'Hold him off. Whoever he is, hold him off, Karl. Do one honourable thing in your pathetic lie of a life.'

Karl steps out of the bath and I run into my old bedroom at the back of the house. I slam the door shut, go the window and try to push up the bottom of the stiff sash. I hear Karl lurching towards the stairs and the sound of footsteps on the risers.

'Ah Mr Rafferty. How nice to you see you again so soon. Now, where is your good lady wife so that we can start the search? That is why you're here, I take it, to help us find the will. Cops let you out, did they? Couldn't they pin anything on you?' says a cold voice on the landing. Something in me recognizes the tone. I am sure it is the man on the train and later on the phone. It must be Nicholas Grainger.

The window will not move and I look around for something to lever it open with.

'Stand out of my way now, Mr Rafferty,' says the same voice in the hallway.

Frustrated at my attempt to get out I grab my old bedroom chair and fling it at the window glass. The noise will surely give me away but I think I might be able to jump onto the kitchen roof and escape through the back.

I can hear a fight on the landing, the sound of punches and thumps.

'Get out of my way,' the voice is shouting.

'You won't get past me. I won't let you through until you can tell me where you are holding Jack,' Karl is shouting.

I pick my way through the bits of glass that are stuck to the window frame and climb out onto the sill. I jump onto the kitchen roof and find myself sliding down onto the gutter, grazing myself with bits of random glass along the way. I grab onto the gutter, hoping it will hold my weight, turn backwards and leap into the back garden. I can hear what I think is the sound of someone falling down the stairs. My feet hit the ground. It is only then that I remember I have no shoes on. Barefoot, I start to run.

25

The Graveyard

I SCAMPER THROUGH THE garden and out the back gate. Running down the lane at an unsteady pace, just as I am about to turn right onto Hill Street, I remember the bike and pull it upright. There is blood coming from my legs and arms but I cannot stop to check and stem its source. I mount quickly, cycle downhill and pick up speed. The old metal pedals pierce my feet as I push on them. It is easy for me to ignore physical pain. My mind is focused on getting far away from here. The darkness covers me but one of the front mudguards is rusting and chafing at the wheel. I must have bent it when I dumped the bike before. It is noisy in the stillness of the village.

I look back and can see someone come out of the front door of Hill Street but can't make out who it is. I can see the shape of a Land Rover outside the front door and see the figure approaching it. It must be Nicholas Grainger.

It looks like the car that Charlie used to drop me at the station this morning. That train station run seems so long ago now.

Fear grips me as I see the shadow of Nick get into the Land Rover. He must be coming after me.

I cycle past the Church of Ireland grounds and notice the side entrance into the graveyard. I know as soon as he starts the Land Rover he will catch up with me. Leaving the bike against a lamppost I go around the bend of the graveyard and climb over the waist-high stone wall. I slump down behind it and hide, thinking how best to get to the estate entrance where I am supposed to meet Frank. Doubt is all invasive in my thoughts. Am I doing the right thing going to meet him?

The Land Rover starts up and I hear the furious sound of it over-revving. First it comes down the street towards me and I curse the bike, thinking it will give me away. It passes me and goes on to the village square, turns and comes back towards me, going at a painstakingly slow pace, full headlights on; it's going to pass me again.

I crouch down further into the wall. I close my eyes and hear it pass me for the second time and then the sound recedes. I think I might be in the clear but the crisp night air carries the revving sound closer again. He is coming back. He must have turned again at the top of the village and is still searching.

My legs are throbbing and I start to pick small pieces of glass out of them wondering whether I have left a blood trail that will be discernible in this light. The Land Rover passes by the wall again. I hold my breath as I hear the engine cut out and stop. I hear the door open and soon the sound of leather-soled boots are on the pavement. I know he is approaching. I peak through the gaps in the stones. He stops on his way towards the wall. Something has caught his eye. It's my bike. He slowly walks over to it and looks around. The bank file is still attached to the back carrier and I can see him free it and examine it under a street light. I think I have given myself away.

As quietly as I can, I get down on my belly, crawling along the grass spaces between the graves. I am careful to take complete cover every few minutes behind a headstone, to stop and listen for the warning of footfall.

After what seems like a long time crawling I get to the darkest part of the graveyard and wait a few moments, clutching onto a gravestone on my hunkers and trying to stop breathing so fast.

The Land Rover moves now but only to get a better view of the graveyard. He has turned it at right angles to the street. He gets out again and leaves the headlights on. I see his shadow searching the inside of the stone wall where I had hidden only a few moments ago. I can make him out as he pulls open the half moon iron gate.

He is now in the churchyard. He has a torch. I stay crouched and hidden, afraid to move and risk breaking the silence.

But his search is interrupted by the noise of angry voices. The car is blocking the road and another wants to pass. The row must have woken some of the villagers as I can see bedroom lights being turned on. There's talking now, but I can't make out the muffled voices from this distance. Nick's shadow turns from the stone wall, goes out the gate, shouts at someone, gets back into the Rover and starts it up. I notice the sound of gears shifting, first, second, third, it picks up speed as it leaves behind my hiding wall and keeps going. The engine sound begins to fade and not return. He is heading off in the direction of the estate.

A feeling of relief comes over me and with it a strange peace, but I remember that this is usual whenever I am in a burial ground. I begin to calm. As a child I would wander around this very place. We used to visit Julian. I would spend hours reading the inscriptions on the headstones, fascinated that whole generations of families could be buried in the same plot, romanticizing about the tragic deaths of the young, learning off the semi-eroded epitaphs carved on old granite stone. I always found it oddly comforting to imagine that I might end up here, in this quiet peaceful place.

The yew trees sway in a gusty breeze; the blackness of the night begins to recede and gives way to intermittent moonlight.

Coldness runs through me and I shiver as I let go of the headstone to rub my bare arms in a vain attempt to warm myself. It is only then that I notice the inscription;

In Loving Memory of Edgar Royston
Born 1917 Died 1989
Loving husband of Katherine
Loving father to Julian (RIP) and Helen

I have been here before but have not seen the headstone with my father's name on it. The last time I was here was when the grave was freshly dug to accommodate his coffin.

'One of the last to get in,' Mrs Molloy said at the time.

I justified not coming back to visit by saying that I preferred to hold a real person like Edgar in my memory rather that to be reminded of his presence with cold, polished stone. In truth, I could never face his grave. I didn't want to think of his body lying cold and rotting in the earth.

But how strange it is that I should find myself here and that the grave of my father should give me shelter; that he should be buried beneath my feet?

Closing my eyes, I imagine Edgar again and wonder what he would do now. More calmness comes to me now, a strange calmness this time, almost calculating. I can feel a strength in me now that wasn't there before.

The memory of my last visit to Edgar comes back to me, shooting on the estate in the pheasant season. But this time I do not recall the words of our conversation.

I can only see my father's guns.

26

The Wall

I DECIDE TO MAKE for the estate through the back fields of the village hoping that the lanes are as I remember them, that the developers have not come and altered the intricate labyrinth of the townscape.

I find the back gate of the churchyard and, as I go through it, the sky begins to darken. The wind picks up, cold and biting. The sky is full of angry black clouds. Thunder greets me as I hurry across another lane. The sky opens up and the rain begins, sharp and cutting on my skin, filling up the gullies quickly, turning the ground underfoot to soft brown mud. I had forgotten the geography of the village; Cillindara is nestled between two large mountains and is renowned for its rain all year around.

In my head I keep referring back to the conversation with Karl. He married me because he did a deal with my mother. Perhaps she could not bear Jack to be brought up without a father. But to pawn me off on one of her rejects is incomprehensible. I cannot bear to think of the two of them scheming together.

Luckily, I can still make out the off-road route I used to take back to Cillindara on the nights that I would sneak out to the village. Now there are new estates of brown and redbrick modern houses in the most unlikely places, behind the national school yard, in the grounds of the village doctor's house. There is the usual incongruous mixture of townhouses and apartments, duplexes, semis and detached. I glimpse bare green plots that developers left behind, an excuse of a playground for a new generation of children. I wonder what the market value of the land at Cillindara is worth. It is common knowledge that when prices maxed out in Dublin there was still money to be made in the country. To be truthful I had thought of this myself. I recall toying with the idea of getting all the Roystons together to rationalize the potential of their inheritance, but I had dismissed the notion as it would have been no benefit to me. The prospect of dealing with any of the Roystons was not one that I welcomed. Is it conceivable then that was why they all resented me so much? Did they all know that I was a first-line blood relative? Nevertheless I had thought of it, I had day-dreamed of buying them all out and making a handsome profit. Does that make me my mother's daughter? 'Cut out of the same cloth', that's what Charlie said this morning.

But no, I am not her; I am not like her. I have a son, my lovely boy Jack, and I will care for him. I will get him back.

Thankfully the basic layout of the paths has not been changed and at the end of Cows Yard Lane I slide under a barbed-wire fence and scurry across a wet field. It is full of big tyre trenches and sparse clumps of buttercups trying to cling onto their survival. The field has been savaged; the preparation of yet another site. The mud makes it a welcome relief for my bare feet but it makes me slip and I precariously reach the shelter of the forest on the other side.

It's a pine forest, dark even on a sunny day, planted on the side of a small hill. It is still not light and I am plunged into deeper darkness as I make my way through the floor of brown needles and try to remember where my father stored his guns. They should still be in the tack room under lock and key. Out of breath, I reach the top of the hill and can see the forest clearing.

I stop and hide to assess the land in front of me. One big ripe field of hay and, at the edge of it, rows of wild foxgloves still asleep in the relentless rain. Beyond the field is the small road that surrounds Cillindara land, and then the familiar high old estate wall on the other side. My mobile bleeps again and I open another text from Frank.

Are you OK? Are you on your way?

I look at it and decide not to answer; my tactic is to use what little advantage I have, that is, the element of surprise.

The old entrance through a gap in the wall comes clear into my view. I opt to take the route around the field, close to the hedges, to afford me some cover. I disturb black crows from their early morning foraging and they fly up out of the hay in groups, flapping wings and squawking.

I am wet, cut, muddy and bedraggled. Yet I am driven on; I will find Jack. He will be alive. I have to believe this.

As I get closer to the edge of the field I still can't see Frank waiting. I cross the road hesitantly and make my way along the stone wall looking for the elderberry tree that hides the gap from the roadside. I find it and climb through, immediately crouching down again for cover. I wait in silence and listen to the sound of the rain falling on the leaves of the oak trees. The ground smells wet and sweet.

After a few seconds I hear a whisper.

'Helen, Helen, is that you?'

It's Frank's voice so he is here, but to what purpose? Is he with me or with that shadow Nick?

'Helen, it's OK you can come out, I'm on my own.'

I slowly come to standing and he emerges, smiling at first but shocked then at my appearance.

'Christ, Helen, what did you do to yourself?'

I am in no mood to talk about the way I look.

'Never mind about me, Frank. Start talking. What exactly is your involvement in this? Why didn't you tell me more about the business deals you had with my mother? Were you blackmailing her? Is this what this is all about? Are you in on this with Nick Grainger?'

Frank takes a step back and raises his two hands above his shoulders, palms open.

'Whoa, hold on there, not so fast. I will explain everything. Thanks for coming, for trusting me enough.'

'I don't trust you one inch, Frank Callan.'

Then he motions with his head to a place behind him and I notice a glint in between the trees. Frank follows my eyes.

'They're guns; go on, have a look,' he says.

I step closer and see a rifle and a shotgun leant up against a tree trunk.

'Where did you get these?'

'I broke into the tack room. Go on, carry them if you like, they're loaded but the safetys are on.'

I go towards the guns and pick them up carefully. They are my father's all right. A .22 left over from his days in the army and a shotgun for the pheasant shoots on the estate. I pick up the rifle and run my fingers down the cold steel barrel. When my touch reaches the mahogany on the butt it is warm by comparison. This is the gun that I learned to shoot with. I click open the chamber and see the brass end of two bullets. I shut the chamber and test the sights. I put the safety back on. In a more hurried fashion I check the shotgun and then hold one gun in each hand weighing them up. I wonder should I carry both of them, or give one to Frank. The shotgun is lighter, but I cannot let go of the rifle. I prefer its precision. I look back at Frank, look down at the guns and then throw him the shotgun. He catches it and smiles.

'I don't blame you, by the way, for not trusting me. But we've got to get going. We'll talk along the way.'

'Get going where, Frank? What's going on?'

'We're going up to the summer-house. That's where he has Jack.'

27

The Deal

'WHAT? WHY DIDN'T YOU tell me? Is he all right? He hasn't been harmed?'

'No, he's fine; he's just tied to a chair with him on one side and Charlie on the other back to back.'

'Are you sure he's all right?'

'At the moment he's fine. It's Charlie I am more worried about. Nick roughed him up a bit.'

'What? He beat up an old man? But why didn't you get them out?'

'Derek, our friend from the train, and another lad called Joe are guarding them and Nick thinks I'm helping him, that's why. Come on.'

'Who is Derek really, who's the other guy?'

'Just some lowlife that Nick picked up. We know that they were the ones who picked up the boys on the motorbikes from the drawing. Nick must have deliberately got Derek to plant the infor-mation about Ballytain to us on the train.'

We are making our way through the oak forest now, uphill, the ground is soggy and slippy. I fling the rifle across my shoulder and pull on roots of bracken to hoist me up the verdant dark clay banks. The ground smells sweet and rich and the soil lodges underneath my fingernails. There is a carpet of bluebells and wild garlic on the ground. I breathe their woodland scent. For the first time I truly admit to myself that this is my homeland. I am back.

The going is tough as Frank says we have to stay off the main pathway and go through the forest under cover. We reach a little ledge and catch our breath.

'We have to hurry. I don't want Nick to get back before us. It all started years ago – remember I told you about growing the weed on the estate?'

'Yes.'

'Well, I could never quite fathom Charlie's attitude towards it. I mean, not only did we not get into trouble, but he was nice to us about it. He even came up with other, legal alternatives, for us to make a few bob. What I didn't realize at the time was that they weren't his ideas.'

'Whose were they?'

'I presumed they were your mother's, but now I am not so sure. Anyway, we went off to London and put that episode behind us but when we got back we naturally made contact with Charlie again. And so it started.'

'What started?'

'The business relationship with your mother. She came up with the notion that she sell us some land and we were only too eager to get a chance to get into the building game for ourselves so we jumped at it.'

'What land did she sell you?'

'You know what they used to call the poppy field at the end of the estate near the town?'

'Yes, of course, I know it.'

'She did a deal with us whereby all we had to do was build the houses and we could pay her for the land after the houses had been sold.'

'But you didn't realize it wasn't her land to sell, right?'

'You have it there, we were green young eejits at the time. We respected her and old man Royston when he was alive. It never crossed our minds that she would have duped us. We just signed whatever documents were put in front of us and didn't even have our own solicitor. We never had any idea that what we were doing would land us in such a legal mess. All we saw was a good deal so we grabbed it. You've got to remember this was the early nineties, just before the boom, it gave us a big head start.'

'Then what?'

'A couple of years later, Nick and I were still working together, she came to us again, through Charlie, and wanted to know if we would take up an option to buy all the land on the estate outright on her death. Naturally we had no idea that she only had caretaker rights. She claimed you were always going to get the house, with a curtilage of about five acres, and whatever was left of the proceeds of the land sale. She said she had been left with very little income by your father and she just needed the cash.'

'Yes, that part is true.'

'So we paid her a hundred and fifty thousand for the right of first refusal and a ten per cent discount on the market price at the time of her death. It was a big sum of money at the time, but one that we both were able to afford as we were doing well at the building game in Dublin. Unfortunately, Nick and I had a big bust up and things started to go wrong after that.'

That was the large sum lodged into the account that I saw in the bank statement.

'Why, what happened?'

'Nick had a high lifestyle, fast cars, overseas trips, golf junkets, race horses not to mention his wives and mistresses. The wealthier he got the more he spun out of control. His first wife did well out of him but his second wife really cleaned him out in court. On top of that he got burnt on a development in Malaga. Finally I cut my ties with him completely as he was dragging every project we got involved in into debt. Even with all his bad luck I couldn't work out where all the damn money was going and then I latched on that he was into the old marching powder. Do you know what I mean?'

'Yes, I do know exactly what you mean, Frank. Go on.'

'On top of being in financial trouble he had problems getting insurance on his sites as he had such a bad safety record. He always had high notions for himself, but in the last couple of years between the booze and whatever else he's on, he has got completely out of control. I've tried to dig him out here and there, passing him small sites when they came my way, but he has just blown the lot. He's come to the end of the line. The smart money got out of Dublin before 2006 and diversified. He didn't. There is still money to be made outside the capital and he knows that. He has no assets left and no bank in the country will extend him finance. This is his only way out. He thinks that if he can make that cock-eyed deal stick he'll be back in the clover. I've tried to persuade him otherwise. I wasn't interested in harassing a dying woman, for God's sake, but there is no reasoning with him. He has got very bitter and blames everyone except himself for the way his life has turned out. He particularly blames your mother.'

'Get to the point, Frank, we're nearly there. What has this got to do with Jack?'

'Our investment in the estate was basically the only thing he had left. Funny thing was that the more experienced I got in the building game the more suspicious I became of the whole land deal. At the back of my mind I always knew I should have had it checked out and then, as things do, events took over before I got a chance. Last year the National Roads Authority planned a new ring road near Cillindara and that meant the price of the land on the estate could quadruple overnight if we could get it re-zoned from agricultural to residential. The problem was getting the deal to stand up.'

'How much money are you talking about here, Frank? Quantify it.'

'At the time we did the original deal the land would have been worth over one and a half million punts; just with the passage of time it's now worth ten million euros, but with the road going through I'd say forty million euros would be a conservative estimate.'

'Jesus, I had no idea.'

'Nick began hassling me to see if he could start again with another site on the estate, but at this stage I seriously doubted the authenticity of the deal. I got in touch with Charlie and realized she was sick. It was awkward. Nevertheless, we came down a couple of months back, ostensibly to see if we could get her to help us in a re-zoning application, but the true purpose was to copper fasten the original deal.

'This time, I brought my solicitor with me and then it all came out. Not only could we not hold her to the deal to buy out the estate land but we found out that the original houses we built on in the poppy field haven't got proper title. For some fortunate reason not one of them has been sold on yet. But as soon as one house-holder decides to sell and the title is found to be corrupt we will be in for a very costly legal battle. I was all on to take a step back, let her die in peace and then try and sort it out amicably with the legal owners of the estate. That's what this is all about, Helen.'

'Oh my God. What a mess. Why didn't you tell me from the beginning?'

'I wasn't sure how you would react. I stupidly thought I could sort it out myself before it got this far.'

'Did you confront my mother?'

'Yes, Nick insisted; the legals were involved too. She said she would persuade you to hand over the land where the houses are built for a nominal fee.'

'And I would have, no problem, if you had come to me, if I had only been asked. But all of this would have been dependent on me knowing that I was going to inherit. That's it really. She couldn't tell me because it would mean admitting Edgar was my father.'

'That's when I suggested getting you down here yesterday. I was hopeful we would be able to sort out the whole mess ourselves.'

'What about the money? Your original hundred and fifty grand?'

'Well, there's the sting in the tail. She offered us the art collec-tion in lieu of the land claiming that the paintings would realize enough to compensate us for our initial investment and give us a healthy profit. She said that she had accumulated some of the pieces herself and that others had been left to her personally by your father, that they weren't part of the estate.'

'Yes, that bit is true, and did you accept?'

'No, not initially. Nick was dead set against it as he was banking on getting the land to bring him back to the income levels he had got used to. He has continued to run up debts on the strength of it. I knew he was losing it but I swear to God, Helen, I didn't know he would take it this far. I persuaded him to do nothing until we had the pieces checked out, talked to you, got a proper legal opinion.'

'And?'

We are nearing the summer-house now and Frank makes a gesture for me to be silent. Then, as we are standing close by each other, he whispers, 'All forgeries, the entire fucking art collection, not a single one is genuine. Karl sold off the lot and Nick has gone ballistic.'

28

The Plan

I STUMBLE BACKWARDS INTO Frank as I try to take in what he has just said. I cannot understand why she did this. The entire collection forged? No wonder the atmosphere in my house earlier between Frank and Karl was hostile. Frank knew that Karl had been in on it. But to learn that my mother and my husband managed to destroy years of the Royston art collection and her own is baffling. She couldn't have been paying Karl all that money. It doesn't make sense. There are plenty of ways of getting money if you are asset rich and income poor. She could have borrowed against the art collection, or come to me. That's it, of course, she would never have asked me for anything, nor I her; we did have that in common. And if she had come to me she would have had to admit that Edgar was my father. For some reason she had held back that vital piece of information.

'But, Frank, what on earth has this got to do with the will?'

'That's what I don't understand and Nick doesn't trust me now so he's not telling.'

'Why doesn't he trust you?'

'Don't you get it, Helen? I have been playing a two-handed game all along. I knew he was losing it and when I went to his office the other day to try and reason something out with him, I saw a photo of Jack lying on his desk. That really put the wind up me. Charlie became aware of his instability, if you like, and we decided to get you down here. I didn't believe he was capable of it until I saw the photo of Jack in your house this morning. Then my worst suspicions were confirmed.'

'Why didn't you tell me, if what you are saying is true, why didn't you tell me from the beginning?'

'Helen, you never would have believed me. For God's sake you didn't even know Edgar was your father. That really confused me. Look let's just try to get Jack out of danger, will we? Do you trust me enough to do that?'

'Yes, I guess I have to, Frank.'

We have been scrabbling uphill for about ten minutes now and, as the summer-house comes into view, we slow down and hide behind the low branches of an oak tree. I can see the door and my instinct is to bolt towards it and free my Jack. Frank seems to sense my thoughts.

'Nick must be nearly back by now so we have to be careful,' he says and puts a restraining hand on my arm.

Just then I hear the familiar engine sound. The rain falls softly and silently now, blanketed by the lushness of the trees and ferns. There is a ground mist rising from the forest floor. The Land Rover stops and I can hear the driver door clunk open and then close with a loud bang, I can see Nick getting out and walking towards the summer-house door. He disappears out of our sight.

We sink lower for more cover and stay silent. Then Frank says in a hushed tone, 'This is my plan. We go in there together, unarmed, you claim you know where the will is. It's got to be somewhere in the house. I have already been through Hill Street and it is nowhere there. Lead Nick out and I will try to free Jack and Charlie when he's gone.'

'What? I just walk in there with you with no protection? Come on, Frank, I can't do that. I have told you, I don't know where the will is. I have nothing to offer him. How can I reason with him?'

'Think about it, Helen. It's divide and conquer. As long as he thinks you have what he wants no harm will come to Jack. Make something up about the will. I will deal with the two lads and send Charlie and Jack back to the village the way you came. I know this puts you in an unsafe position with him, but I will go after you with the shotgun as soon as I can.'

'What if he's armed, Frank? What then?'

'Nick is unstable. I have told you that. If we go in with the guns all hell could break loose. I have a fishing knife tied to my leg if things get nasty, but let's keep the guns out of it for the moment.'

I agree with him reluctantly. It's a plan that might work and I don't have an alternative. We store the guns underneath some ferns and begin to make our way over to the entrance. As we are about to approach the door I stop dead in my tracks. I can feel the cold steel barrel of a gun at my back.

'Ah, Mrs Rafferty, I presume, how good of you to join us,' says a voice from behind me.

29

The Surprise

'NOW TURN AROUND SLOWLY, hands in the air. Slowly mind, we don't want any accidents, do we?' continues the voice.

I turn and face the man I remember as Nick Grainger. His hair is dark still but it is now greying around the temples; his teeth are yellowed and stained; his face has weathered badly and there is a smell of stale whiskey from his breath. What happened to the handsome man I once knew?

Yet he still stands proud before me, a distasteful cockiness in his stature. He throws his head back and breathes in sharply a couple of times through his nostrils. There is something aristocratic about him that, strangely, reminds me of my father. He smiles and in an instant I can read him. This man is on a bender and he is either totally insane, extremely dangerous or both.

As I square up to him he moves the shotgun and points it directly at my forehead. He stares at me as he takes the safety off and cocks the trigger.

'Easy on now, Nick. Helen's come here to sort this out. For God's sake, man, be reasonable,' says Frank.

I look into Nick's eyes and know there will be no reason with him: he has gone past the point of logic.

Someone passes behind my back. I am too frightened to turn my head to look, and then I hear another gun being cocked and I know that Frank, too, is at gunpoint.

'Nick, get him to take that thing off me,' says Frank.

'You don't fool me anymore, Frank. You were in this with her all along, weren't you?'

'What are you talking about, Nick?'

'You warned her I was coming to Hill Street. There is no other way she could have got out. You turned on me, Frank, and led her here.'

'Please take the gun off her; let's all work this out together. You do realize you have committed a felony? No amount of money is going to get you out of this. Now this is your chance to sort it out before you get a gaol sentence.'

'Move,' he says and makes us go back the way we came. We go back into the thickness of the forest and I wonder now if this will be how it ends. Is my body to be found here in the thicket of the forest of Cillindara?

'Tie them up,' Nick says to the boy behind Frank and I recognize Derek as he ties me to the trunk of a tree. I try to catch his eye but he avoids looking at me.

I manage to glance over at Frank. This was not part of the plan. Things are not going well.

I want to scream but Derek puts a tape on my mouth and prevents it. I sink down onto the ground. Frank is stood up and tied to a tree not far from me. His mouth is not taped.

'Nick, what are you thinking? Helen will tell you whatever you want to know.'

'What am I thinking? What were you thinking when you got me involved with her mother, the old bitch … don't you remember the site and the legal mess we are in? Ten bloody houses built on land that we didn't even own. You were the one who did the deal with her. So don't get all sanctimonious with me.'

'We were young. How were we to know that Katherine didn't own the land? Sure I had never even heard the word conveyance before that and neither had you. I thought lawyers were all sound back then. It was an honest mistake, one that I will gladly pay for. C'mon, Nick, what's happened to you? You don't want any harm to come to the child now, do you?'

'Ah Frank, how kind of you to offer to pick up the bill; to have me humiliated further by trying to bail me out. Are you going to give me twenty million? Is that what you're offering?'

Frank shakes his head.

'I didn't think so. Half this land is rightfully mine and I intend to get it.'

'We can go through legal channels. This is not the way to sort this out. For God's sake, what possessed you to take the child?'

'Shut up, Frank, I've listened to you for long enough.' I see him take a hip flask from his pocket and swig a mouthful of what I presume is whiskey. Frank is still pleading with him, trying to reason, but I know that this will do no good. He walks over to Frank raging, angry beyond control. He holds the shotgun by the barrel and whacks Frank across the face with the butt of it.

'Shut up, I said, or else it will be your girlfriend next. Tape him up, Derek. I don't want to hear another word from him.'

Frank half falls to the ground but the ropes prevent him from actually reaching it. I can see blood coming from his head. Derek goes over and tapes his mouth.

Nick approaches me and kneels down on the forest floor so that he is at my level.

'You know I always liked you, Helen. Felt that you and I were kindred spirits if you get my meaning. My mother was a single parent, too. Did you know that?'

No, I shake my head furiously, but I don't get his meaning I cannot anticipate what this man is going to do next.

'The only difference was I didn't get rescued from the local national school and sent off to England like you. No, I had to put up with the taunts from the Brothers instead. Calling me a bastard, asking me where my father was, if my mother would put it out there for a few bob. No public-school education for me. I didn't get the chance to be brought up in the gentry like you.'

What is he going on about? What relevance has my education got to do with anything? Was he jealous of me, is that it?

'It was unfortunate for you that the old bird died so quickly before she had a chance to sort this out. You know she adored the boy, which was plain to anyone who knew her. You must understand that the way she played her hand it was the only leverage I had over her. No, life certainly doesn't go according to plan, does it, Helen?' he says, and prods me with the barrel of the shotgun.

I sit with my gaze fixed at him, terrified, unable to respond.

'Now we have to work out carefully what we are going to do in our present situation, don't we?' he says and prods me again this time harder in the chest.

I nod furiously, trying not to annoy him further.

'Helen, you don't mind if I call you Helen, do you? If you could see Charlie you'd know that I have tried my best to get that man to co-operate with me. As far as I can tell he may actually have been telling the truth but unfortunately the poor old bugger passed out on me before we could get to the bottom of this. That leaves me in a bad position. Did you know it was Frank's idea to get you down here in the first place? Charlie was following his instructions? Did you know that, or was it something lover boy over there omitted to tell you?'

Lover boy? Boyfriend – is the attraction between Frank and I so obvious?

I glance over at Frank and his eyes meet mine momentarily before they drop to the floor. He has told me this already.

'But do know why he wanted you here?'

I shake my head again.

'He wanted you here because you were the only person your mother would talk to, the only person whom she would tell where the last copy of the will is. And that, my dear Helen, is what this is all about. She did her best, the old bitch, bless her, to make it look like herself and your father died intestate. She even got that old incompetent solicitor of hers to destroy the second copy so that she held the only one.

'Now, Helen,' he says, and he prods me again. This time he puts the barrel down the neck of my T-shirt and digs it into my bra. 'Now do you see what I have here?' and he produces what looks like vials of some sort of medication and needles from his jacket pocket.

My pupils dilate.

'Oh don't worry, it's just some of Mummy's medicine. A touch of morphine to help her get through the night no doubt. Helen, tell me, have you any idea how much of this would kill a child, a half-grown child like your boy Jack?'

I shake my head furiously.

'Mmm, neither do I really, to tell you the truth, but let's see now, three doses would probably do the trick. A nice peaceful ending, no pain, just enough to make him go out on a high note, if you see what I mean.'

He begins to laugh. I close my eyes and begin to cry. It can't end like this, it can't.

'Oh I'm so sorry, Helen I didn't mean to upset you.'

He begins to touch my face now, pawing me, his hands maul my breasts. His hands sink lower and he touches me between my legs.

'It could always be worse, Helen,' he whispers.

He continues to grope. His hand unzips my trousers. I want to be sick. To my relief he stands up and backs away slightly.

'Now you know and I know that your mother dearest told you where the will is, didn't she?'

I nod my head wondering what I am going to make up to get out of this.

'I am going to take off your gag Helen, and when I do you are going to tell me exactly where it is. Isn't that right, Helen?'

I nod again in assent.

He pulls the tape off my mouth sharply.

At first I gulp in a couple of breaths.

'Yes, yes, I will tell you, but first you have to let me see Jack.'

I feel a sharp blow across my face and know that I too have been hit with the butt of the shotgun. The side of my face stings with pain.

'Don't think you can do any deals with me, Helen Royston, you little bitch.'

'I know my mother duped you and I am willing to compensate you. Anything, anything you want from the estate you can have. I swear it. I just don't see how finding this will is going to help you.'

He laughs again, a loud belly laugh that makes me feel nauseous. He comes closer to me so that I can feel his warm, stinking breath on my face and says, 'Didn't it ever occur to you, Helen, that you're not the only bastard your father sired?'

30

The Last Visit

I LOOK UP AT HIM in shock. This news is devastating. Nick Grainger is my half-brother and although I have not worked out the implications of it I know that this changes everything. I would never have anticipated this but now the search for the will is beginning to make sense. This is my father's son. That's why I saw the resemblance in him.

I can hear Frank making a muffled sound of surprise and I look over at him. Blood has flowed down the back of his skull and is caking on his face. For the first time I see fear in his eyes.

'Did you hear that, Frank?' taunts Nick. 'Your girlfriend here is my half-sister. Now do you get it, you canny bastard? All these years and you never knew I was part of the Royston royalty, did you, Frank? You never copped it. Didn't you ever wonder why old Charlie didn't go to the guards all those years ago? Well, I'll tell you why, Frankie dearest, he saw the Royston in me, the resemblance to Edgar was unmistakable and he went to Katherine with his suspicions.'

He's on a roll now, taking another swig from his hip flask, pacing up and down between me and Frank. He takes a torn-up piece of a magazine out of his pocket, turns aside and then I hear him sniff the contents. Then he turns his head again to my direction.

'Daddy dear, had to 'fess up then, didn't he? Had to tell your dear mother that he had another little dirty secret. You didn't see that one coming, Ms High and Mighty Royston, did you?'

He pokes the shotgun into me again. It hurts and I recoil back as far as I can towards the tree trunk. This annoys him further and his tone changes from one of mockery to acidic clarity.

'There was to be a family announcement, Helen, at the old man's seventieth, but you didn't bother your arse turning up, did you? Couldn't even give the old man that final courtesy.'

Oh God no, that's what Edgar was trying to tell me the last day we went shooting.

'It must have been all too much for him, so he decided to drop dead rather than acknowledge his only living son. Not a good move in terms of family relations. What do you think, Sis?'

That's why she didn't tell me. Oh sweet Jesus, it is now so clear. She would have had to explain that Nick was my half-brother.

'Now, I am going to ask you one last time where the will is. Charlie told me that your mother told you before she died, that was the purpose of your visit. You can't hide it any longer. Where is it?' He begins to spit saliva as the words come out of his mouth. He walks over to me and slaps me hard across the face again this time with the back of his hand. He is losing control. I know that I have to come up with a location for the will and desperately try to recall the visit I had with my mother.

'It's in her study,' I blurt out.

'Exactly where in her study? I have already been through the place with a fine-tooth comb. Where is it?'

'It's hidden in the back of the bookcase,' I lie.

Nick kneels down to my level and grabs hold of my jaw.

'You'd better be telling the truth, Ms Royston, or else all of this will come to a very nasty end. Do you get my meaning?'

I look at him coldly and fleetingly think how different things could have been. My past is a murky mess as no doubt his is, but I must somehow shake that off and emerge stronger than this menace that lies before me.

'Yes, yes, I understand you completely.'

He stands up straight and assumes a haughtiness that sits uneasily with his unkempt appearance.

'Good. We'll untie you then, shall we, and go hither to your mother's study?'

He loosens the ties that bind me to the tree and helps me to my feet. My legs are like jelly under me and it takes me moments to stand. My hands are still bound behind my back. He turns me around and digs the barrel of the shotgun into the back of my neck. He shoves me towards the forest path again.

'Derek,' he says looking over his shoulder, 'keep a close eye on our friend Frank while I am gone now, won't you? We wouldn't want any accidents to happen, would we?'

He marches me out of the thickness of the forest, past the Land Rover and down the well-worn path. The sky opens up again and the rain comes down in gusty torrents. As I slide and slip under his direction I wonder how I am going to get out of this. I try desperately to recall the exact words my mother said when I went to see her. At the time I thought she was too drugged to be making any sense and I had dismissed her words without thinking out their possible meaning. She had been very dopey and her words had been slurred.

Think, Helen, think, I keep telling myself, as Nick pushes me on towards the main house and I relive the last visit I made to the summer-house.

'It's me mother it's me.'

'I'm so glad you came to see me, darling, after all this time. Now sit, sit on the bed I have to tell you something ... something ...' *The effort of those few words of conversation seemed to have made her exhausted and she had closed her eyes. I sat and I had thought that she was sleeping but after a few moments she opened her eyes again and smiled.*

'You know now don't you?'

'I know what, Mother?'

'Why. Why I couldn't tell you before.'

I had no idea what she was talking about then so I had just played along with her, shocked at the physical state that she was in.

'Yes, Mother, I know. Now try and rest, Mother, you look tired.'

'Tired, do I? It's the nurse, you know, she keeps giving me the sleeping injections. Too many I think.'

I had looked over at a figure in the white uniform and realized then that I wasn't alone with her. Of course there would be someone with her in her advanced state of cancer. The nurse saw me and lifted her finger to her nose and I knew the injections were morphine. The same morphine that now might kill my Jack.

What else did she say? Remember, Helen, remember, I try to coax myself.

I was sitting on the bed beside her. She lay back, as if spent and I found myself stroking her hair. I used to do that as a child in Hill Street. But now her whole body had shrunk and her face had become frail as a bird's. Her eyes hollowed back into their sockets. She had a deathly grey complexion and a small sliver of saliva dribbled from her lips. I stopped stroking her hair to take a tissue and wipe the corners of her mouth.

She looked strangely childlike.

'Don't stop, Helen, don't stop. You haven't done that in a long time.'

I began to stroke her hair again, softer with my touch this time, almost caring.

'No, Mother I haven't, have I?'

It was an odd thing that myself and my mother were never openly affectionate in public. There was never any kissing or hugging. But at night, on our own in Hill Street, her guard would be let down and if she was in good humour I would be allowed to come into her room and play with her paste jewellery and lipstick. Then she would give my hair a hundred strokes with her silver-handled hairbrush and I would do the same for her. It was the only secret we ever had between us. When I was finished she would sometimes let me sleep in her bed with her, but always before I woke in the morning she would be up and dressed for work and the softer mother that I sometimes knew at night would be gone only to be replaced with a cold angry hardness. I didn't want to care for her again now.

She drifted off while I was stroking and I sat until again I thought she slept.

I got up to leave but she held onto me and whispered,

'He'll never get it.'

'Get what, Mother? Who will never get it?'

'That boy, that horrible boy.'

'Are you talking about Jack, Mother?'

She smiled at the mention of his name.

'No, no, not Jack, not my lovely boy Jack … the other one. But just so you know it's at the back of the forest, that's what I wanted to tell you. That's where I kept it all these years.'

'What's at the back of the forest, Mother?'

'You know now where it is. Don't forget, will you?'

'No, Mother, I won't forget,' I said.

I had no idea what the conversation had meant.

'I'll see you tomorrow, Mother, all right. I'll come again in the morning to stroke your hair. Would you like that, Mother?'

'You know I'd like that more than anything Helen, more than anything in the whole world. You were always a good girl, Helen, always a good girl. I was wrong, so very wrong not to tell you.'

'Not to tell me what, Mother, what?'

Again there was no response from her. Her mind seemed to be unable to discern reality from her drug-induced imaginings. There was a silence then and I looked towards the nurse as if to bid her nearer. I knew then that she was very far gone but wouldn't admit it even to myself.

'All right, Mother, you sleep now, you need your rest,' I had said as the nurse swapped places with me. *Her eyes were closed, her breathing laboured and before I left her bedside I heard it: the death rattle in her chest. I had often heard Mrs Molloy talk about it before, but I had never seriously believed her. It was true then, she was close. The nurse gave me a knowing look.*

I had left the summer-house then, never to fulfil my promise, never to stroke her hair again.

My dalliance into the recent past is interrupted by Nick shoving me in the back with the barrel of the shotgun.

'Keep moving,' he barks.

If only he would stop a second and let me think. All day I have allowed myself to be led along by action and events over which I had no control. Now is the time for me to gather and put my own affairs in order, if only I could think.

It didn't occur to me at the time of my visit to her that she was really trying to tell me where the will was hidden, but now it is obvious. But 'the back of the forest' means nothing to me. Did she hide it somewhere in a forest on the estate? If that is the case I will never find it in time to placate Nick.

The forest path begins to widen and I know we are nearing the main house. Nick pulls at me and turns me around. He looks into my eyes and motions for me to stay silent. I assent. We wait in the darkness of the forest for a few moments. His eyes are focused on the front door. The porch light is on and I can see a Garda pacing up and down. Nick sees him too.

I think about screaming and making a run for it, but Nick could easily shoot me before I make it. As well as that I don't think the Garda will be armed and if I do manage to alert him Nick could have doubled back to the summer-house and harmed Jack before I get to him. Nick pulls me closer to him and covers my mouth with his hand.

'Don't even think about trying anything, Helen, do you understand me? If you take off, I swear to God I will shoot you in the back.'

My decision making is sound then. I am getting to know how this man thinks.

He releases his hand slowly and I turn towards him.

'I'm not going to try anything, I swear.'

Then he balances the shotgun on his shoulder and has the Garda in his sights. The safety is off. Is he seriously thinking of shooting him? I take the risk of putting my hand on the barrel.

'No, don't; if you shoot him we won't be able to repair this situation. There will be no coming back from it. Don't you see I need to know what's in the will just as much as you do? I understand you are angry, but if we get the will there is still a chance to sort this out. Please, Nick, this is not the right way.'

He looks at me and for the first time I see a tired, ageing man. Maybe with the coming of the dawn he is beginning to sober up. I vainly hope that the gravity of the situation will bring him back to his senses.

After a long minute he lowers the gun and says, 'We are going to go around the back of the house and sneak in through the basement. Don't utter a sound.'

'OK, but Mrs Molloy might be there and I don't want her to be alarmed. Let me deal with her and don't point that gun at me when we are in the house.'

He stares at me with contempt.

'You really think that you can order me around? Think that you're the lady of the fucking manor?'

'No, no, it's not that. I just want to get into the house and get the will without involving the Garda. That's all, I swear. You're going to have to untie my hands if you want to pull this off.'

He thinks for a moment and then frees me. As if to reassert his authority he shoves me with the shotgun again and takes a firm grip of my arm. He is hurting me, but the physical pain is nothing compared to the terror that I am feeling. We go off the path and into the thickness of the oak forest and begin to circle around the back. We reach the stable yard and there is no sign of the detectives who were here earlier on. Nick is holding such a firm grip on my arm that it is sore. My face is throbbing from where I have been hit. I have no idea what time it is and if I allowed myself to think about it I would surely be exhausted. But my mind keeps racing, trying to process information, to put this all together as Nick pushes and pulls me across the yard. *He'll never get it* she had said. Now I know she was referring to Nick, but was it the will he wasn't going to get, or his rightful inheritance? Was he entitled to the art collection? Was that it? Oh, Mother, why did you never let me know, know myself and know you?

We scramble across the yard and reach an old tractor. He pulls me down to hide behind it. Checking that the coast is clear we make a dash for the back door.

At first I think the kitchen is empty, but then I see Mrs Molloy coming out of the pantry with flour and eggs in her hands. She is in her dressing-gown. She must have had hardly any sleep at all.

I walk in front of Nick. He sees her and shifts the shotgun behind his back.

When she sees us she drops the eggs to the floor.

'Lord God, girl, what has happened to you? You're in a terrible state. And today of all days, the day of your mother's wake? You'll have to get fixed up now, miss. Pop upstairs and I'll run a nice hot bath for you.'

'I can't get ready yet, Mrs Molloy,' I say.

'Ah, Mr Grainger, what are you doing here? Have you come for the funeral as well?'

Clearly she is perplexed. It was only a couple of hours ago that she was answering questions from me about my mother's business affairs.

'Never mind about that now, Mrs Molloy. There's a Garda outside the front door. Are there any others in the house?' says Nick.

'No, there is no one else here. There were two detectives here earlier on, a man called Malone and I can't remember the other one, but they went off to the village. There is some sort of disturbance there and they were called away. That Garda is from the village. The sergeant sent him up here. He's only a young lad. What's going on with ye at all?'

I decide to placate Mrs Molloy before Nick steps in and makes a mess of it.

'Mrs Molloy, I can't explain everything to you right now, there isn't time, not with the viewing to get ready for. Just listen carefully to me, will you do that for me, for my mother?'

I can see tears well up in her.

'But I don't understand, miss. Where is Charlie? I am here all alone trying to have it the way she would like. It's not right. She was an important woman around here, your mother. I can't do it all myself.'

'Please, Mrs Molloy, you won't have to be here all alone for much longer. Please just do what I ask and everything will work out.'

She wipes her tears away on her apron and agrees.

'We need to get to my mother's study. Can you distract the Garda? Call him down to the kitchen for a cup of tea maybe. He mustn't know we are here. Do you understand?'

'Yes, miss, I was going to ask him in for some breakfast, but I wanted to make a start on the baking first. If … if you are sure that's what you want I'll do it.'

'Yes it is and I'm sure. It's very important now that you don't tell him we are here. Do you promise me, Mrs Molloy?'

'I won't tell him. I'll try to get him down to the kitchen. He won't hear you in the study from here.'

Carefully and quietly the three of us make our way up the kitchen stairs. Nick checks the hallway. There is no one there. The light is still on in the dining-room where my mother lies. It occurs to me that there should be someone in with her there, so that she is not lying all alone, but I cannot go to her. I was never here for her when she was alive and, again, I abandon her in death.

We get to the study and bid Mrs Molloy to go past us on to the front door. We close the study door behind us. I can hear her asking the Garda in for breakfast. Then there is the sound of footsteps on the stairs as they descend into the kitchen.

Nick closes the curtains and turns on the light.

'Get it, get it now,' he motions, 'and let's get out of here.'

I stand frozen unable to work out what to do next. My breathing is heavy and close to panic. I quickly take in the whole room; the desk, the filing cabinet, the bookcase. Then I see my painting of the forest above the fireplace. *It's behind the forest.*

31

The Will

I MOVE TOWARDS THE painting.

'What are you doing? That's not the bookcase. Don't try anything, Helen.'

'It's behind this painting, I am sure of it. I couldn't work out what she was trying to say to me before. Honestly, I'm sure it's behind the painting.'

I approach the fireplace and carefully take down the green and brown canvas. I turn the painting over, hoping, praying that there is something taped onto the back. To my relief I see a large brown envelope.

'Open it.'

My hands are shaking as I carefully take out a foolscap-sized document.

'Read it.'

It is written with ink pen in an old hand. I start to read the opening preamble, lengthy legal jargon.

'Get to the point, the main part; stop wasting time.'

Nick is snarling at me. He is now constantly spitting saliva as he speaks. Nervously I continue.

'I hereby bequeath to my son, Nicholas Grainger, the contents of the house at Cillindara including the family art collection, the furniture and the collection of Irish silver.

I hereby bequeath to my daughter, Helen Royston, the house and lands of the estate of Cillindara to do with as she so wishes.'

'So that's what the old bitch was up to. No wonder she sold off the original art collection. She couldn't even let me have what was rightfully mine. And the land and house is yours, is it, Helen? Forty fucking million euros worth of estate and I am to be left with a forged art collection. What else? Read on.'

'In the event of either sibling predeceasing Katherine Royston the share of their estate will be bequeathed to their issue.'

'What does that mean? Interpret it for me.'

'It means that if I die my share goes to Jack and if you die your share goes to your children.'

'Is that it? Is that the end of it? Give it here.'

He grabs the document from me and reads the last sentence, the part which I had sped read ahead of him. The part I didn't want him to see.

'In the event of Nicholas Grainger or Helen Royston predeceasing Katherine Royston and, there being no issue, the share of either sibling shall revert to the living sibling.'

'Now that means if you and Jack are dead I get the lot. Isn't that right, Helen?'

'Yes, yes, that's it.'

It is easy to see the next logical step of a deranged man. Nick intends to kill me and Jack and claim the entire estate. That's why he needed to check the contents of the will. But how is he going to carry this off without implicating himself as a murderer? Is he going to stage some sort of accident in the summer-house? Is he sober enough to carry this through? A scuffle between siblings that somehow got out of hand? Maybe he will find a way to implicate Frank and Charlie.

Nick puts the will back into the envelope and folds it into his pocket. He steps back from me a little.

'Put the painting back, Helen. We don't want this room to look disturbed.'

What does he mean by that? I have rifled through it already. The evidence is apparent.

'You can have anything you want, Nick, you can have the whole estate. I don't want anything. I'll hand the whole lot over to you.'

'Put it back, Helen, just the way it was.'

I turn to re-hang my painting and, as I do, I feel a hard blow at the back of my head. Pain sears through me and I slump forward. The room is swimming and then everything is black.

32

The End

I AM NOT COMPLETELY knocked out. I have a vague awareness of Nick picking me up and hauling me up over his shoulder. My limbs are loose and dangling. I am so tired now, all I want to do is sleep and sleep and when I wake I want this to be all over. But that's not going to happen and I must try and stay awake. I am not going to let this man murder me and my son so that he can profit.

He's moving now. I know that not because I see it but because with every step he takes the pain in my head hurts more. I can hear his laboured breathing. I try to open my eyes and can see bits of bracken and ferns. I know what he is doing. I know he is bringing me back to the summer-house to die with my Jack. Just when I think I will not be able to stand anymore thumping in my head the moving stops.

'Derek, Derek, where are you?' I can hear him shouting.

I hear a moaning sound. I presume we are back to where I was tied up earlier, close to the summer-house. He swirls around and the dizziness in my head makes me more confused. Quite suddenly he dumps me on the ground. He kicks me and I feign complete unconsciousness.

'What the hell is going on here? Where is Frank?' he is saying.

'He got loose. He had a knife and I didn't see him get free till it was too late.'

'Idiot, I told you to watch him. Where is he now?'

'In there, I think. Look, Mr Grainger, he knocked me out and took me gun. I don't know wha' happened after that.'

'Where's the other one, Joe, have you seen him?'

'No, no, Mr Grainger, I told youse I was knocked out.'

'All right, keep calm. The situation may have changed, but there is a simple way out. We are going to have to stage an accident. Get her, give me two minutes, and follow me into the summer-house. When you get inside put her up against the window that overlooks the valley.'

'Look, Mr Grainger, I didn't sign up for this. It's after goin' too far. First it was just the motorbike snatch, then I nearly got turned over to the guards on the train, then you had me go through that bleedin' shack down the country, but not this. I'm not signing up for this. You're lining yourself up for murdering someone of them. I know it.'

'Do as you're fucking told, boy, or you won't get out of this alive either. Do you understand me?'

There is a momentary quietness. I take it that Derek has consented when I sense a movement close to me.

'Give me two minutes to sort Frank out and then come in after me. You understand, don't you?'

'Yes, Mr Grainger.'

I can hear Nick stomping off and then Derek turns me over. He is trying to work out how to lift me when I open my eyes. I look directly at him.

'You're right, Derek, he is going to murder at least one of us. Now is your only chance to get away. If you leave now I swear I won't implicate you in any of this.'

'You don't understand. Me da works for him. He'll lose his job. Joe is me best mate and he's in there too. I can't just go off and leave him.'

'Are the motorbikes here?'

'Yeah, they're over there.'

'Leave me here and get ready to take off. I'll go in and get Joe out for you.'

Derek considers my proposal.

'How'll you get him out? Youse can hardly walk.'

With enormous effort I make myself get up onto all fours and find my bearings. I force myself to stand, holding onto a branch for support.

'I'm fine, see.'

He is still uncertain.

'You're not a bad lad, Derek. You just got caught up in this. It's not your fault. You can get out of it now. I'll explain everything to your dad. I'll sort it all out.'

Derek looks scared.

'Aw'right, I'm leaving. Tell Joe to meet me where the bikes are. I'll give youse five minutes. That's all. Then I'm outa here.'

At last he scurries off and immediately my pretence at being all right disintegrates and I hug the tree trunk for fear I will fall over. I try to orientate myself. I need to find the guns. I scramble around, lurching from trunk to branch as if drunk, grabbing anything that will give me support. I see the summer-house door and use it as a marker. I back up a little and almost fall downhill. I find the bracken where we hid the guns.

I take the rifle, my head clearing slightly and make my way to the summer-house door.

As I approach it I can hear shouting and scuffles and think carefully about whether I should enter. Because the sliding door opens straight onto the inside room I will be seen straight away and give away whatever advantage I have. I look around and try to think quickly. Out of the corner of my eye I glimpse a piece of steel. There was always a ladder here to scrape off the moss from the flat roof. This must be it. I untangle it from the leaves and as quietly as I can I prop it up against the side wall. I climb up and crawl along the roof felt. I can see an open skylight. I position myself so that I have a view of the inside. Charlie is tied up to a chair and looks unconscious; another young man, presumably Joe, is lurking behind my mother's bed with an eye on the doorway. Frank is shielding Jack, but they are both too close to the main window for my liking. Nick has the shotgun pointed at them.

'Get away from the boy, Frank. I swear to God I'll shoot you.'

Within a second he turns the shotgun to the side of them and fires at the glass. The entire window begins to crack and shatter. The noise is deafening as the glass begins to clatter down the valley. Nick walks closer to them now. His plan is obvious. If he can push Jack off the edge of the summer-house and then get me and push me down after him, he could make it look like an accident. Neither of us will survive that fall.

I remember the new balcony that Charlie said ran all the way around the large window. I pull the ladder up and slowly drag it across the roof. Odd bits of glass keep smashing on the cliff below, a frightening reminder of what Jack will fall into.

'Back up towards the window, Jack. Move across the room, Frank, or you'll go over with him.'

'I'm not leaving him, Nick. Can't you see you're asking the impossible? You can have my death and his on your conscience for the rest of your miserable life,' says Frank.

Then there is another sound. It's the sound of the motorbike starting up. Derek must have decided that five minutes was up. Joe must hear it because the next thing I hear Nick snarl, 'Get back here, Joe, get back.'

I am nearly at the edge of the roof now and I can hear the sliding mechanism of the door. Nick must be distracted. This is my chance. I throw the ladder onto the balcony and shimmy down it as fast as I can. I lose the rifle in the process and it falls behind the edge of the window.

Jack sees me and cries out, 'Mum, Mum, he's going to kill us.'

He runs to me and I hug him tightly. It is so good to be close to Jack again but I cannot let this moment linger.

'It's OK Jack. It's OK,' I say not taking my eyes off Nick.

Nick comes racing back from the door and composes himself before I have time to retrieve the rifle. He exudes contempt.

'Ah, Ms Royston, how good of you to join us. You have saved me the bother of retrieving you from the forest. No doubt Derek took off, did he? The standard of staff is not what it used to be, I'm sure your mother would agree.'

'You're not going to get away with this, Nick.'

'*Au contraire*, little sis. Now I'm going to get you all in one fell swoop.'

'Easy on now, the both of you,' says Frank in a vain attempt to diffuse the situation.

Nick appears uncannily relaxed.

'Did you tell her, Frank? Did you have time while you were on your little jaunt around the country?'

'Tell me what? I know everything now.'

'He always liked you, Helen. That summer when you were here he was always on at me to come up and see you.'

'Please, Nick, not now; I meant to tell her in my own time. Not now, not in front of the boy.'

I look at Frank and I see such pain in his face. What on earth could it be? What is there left to tell?

'He liked you so much, Helen, but you never even looked at him, did you? Poor Frank, he had it bad for years; asking after you at any opportunity; getting old Charlie there to fill him in.'

'Stop it, Nick, stop,' says Frank, but Nick continues, smirking, almost laughing.

'He found you once in Dublin, Helen. You didn't know that, did you? Charlie told us where you hung out. As luck would have it your boyfriend had a party that night. Do you remember now, Helen?'

I look at Frank. He is nodding his head in agreement.

'Were you in Morehampton Road, in Karl's flat?'

'The very one. What can you remember about it, Helen?'

'I was drunk. I went to bed early. I don't remember anything.'

'Just as well then, isn't it?' says Nick, laughing now with gusto.

I look at Frank again. His eyes are pleading, shameful.

'I didn't know. You have to believe me, Helen. You were so lovely. You are so beautiful. Believe me, I never knew. I never knew until today when Charlie told me. He saw the resemblance just as he had seen it between Nick and your father.'

The taunts of him being my boyfriend and lover come back to me. Whispers of friends and relatives swim around in my head. 'No, he's not like his father at all'. 'Jack looks so much like you Helen'. The dream, the dream I had that Karl was making love to me that night of the party flashes before me. The sun is rising through the clouds and I see Frank's face in profile beside Jack's in the weak early-morning light. All of the truth is now finally revealed.

I lose my footing and stumble a little. I hold onto the window frame to prop me up. My physical state, the cuts and bruises on my legs and arms, my bleeding feet, my throbbing head, and my pure exhaustion will not defeat me. But this news might.

'He raped you, Helen. Raped you, when you were passed out. Now what do you think of him? Your hero.'

'It wasn't like that, Nick. You don't understand anything,' I say.

'Well, I certainly could never understand why Frank didn't sue the arse off that old bitch, but sure why would he when he'd—'

'Stop it. Stop it, Nick. I told you I never knew until today. Don't you think I would have done something about it? Do you think I would have left her on her own to have the child? I never would have done that. I thought she was happily married.'

'What are they saying, Mum? I don't understand.' This is Jack.

How can I ever explain this to him? All of my life flashes now before me. In it I have had so many choices. It is true that I have made some bad decisions, that there are things that I regret. Most of all, though, I did not take control. Most of all, I did not see what was in front of me. But now all is clear. I know who I am. My name is Helen Royston and I am the sixth generation of the Royston clan from Cillindara. I have a son, a boy named Jack and he will survive me. Whatever happens he will live.

Frank and Nick are shouting at each other now. There is a sound of Garda sirens in the distance.

'The game's up, Nick. Put the shotgun down. The guards will be here in a few moments,' says Frank.

Nick seems to realize that time is running out.

'I told Detective Malone everything this morning, Nick. They have been on our trail all day. There was no way I could take the risk of leaving Jack's safety to chance.'

'I have the gun, Frank. You are unarmed. I'm not doing time for your little family. Now back up to the edge of the balcony. How ironic that you will finally get to be with your dear Helen in death.'

Frank begins to move towards him. Nick points the shotgun at him and then back to me and Jack. He can't decide who to shoot first.

The words my mother said to me in the dream last night come to me. She said I was to let him go – let him go.

'Jack, remember the chasing game we used to play in the lane? Remember, Jack?'

'Yes, Mum, I remember.'

'Now you are to do it just like you used to. Understand?'

'Yes, Mum.'

'On my count. One.'

Nick turns towards us and I step backwards onto the balcony until my feet can feel the rifle. I know he is expecting the count to reach three. I am willing Jack to understand what I meant.

'Two.'

Jack takes off towards the door. Nick is momentarily surprised. He swings around and points the shotgun at him, aiming to fire, but Frank stands in the way so that Nick does not have a clear line of sight. He pulls the trigger and misses. A piece of plaster falls off the roof. The noise wakes Charlie and there is a groan from the back of the room. He is regaining consciousness. Nick is lurching backwards, not used to the force of the shot, and tries to work out where the sound is coming from. Frank runs over to him and there's a scuffle. I hear the shotgun clatter on the floor. Frank kicks it well out of harm's way. In one swift movement I take up the rifle, click the safety off and balance it on my shoulder.

Nick turns back to me and sees that I am armed. He squares up to me, moving closer.

'You won't do it, Helen. You won't kill your own blood.'

I know that Jack is clear away now. My life, should it be over, has served its purpose. Now it is my turn to laugh.

'You think that I would let you live? You think that there would be a place for you in the Royston clan?'

He is scared now. He knows I have the upper hand.

'Come on, Helen, I wouldn't have harmed you. I'm sorry. It's the years of rejection. I couldn't take it. Have some pity for me.'

'Pity? For a man who dared to take my son? Enough.'

A rifle is more accurate than a shotgun. What's the point in shooting if you don't mean to kill? I aim at the space between Nick's eyebrows.

I press the trigger and fire.

Epilogue

THE SUMMER-HOUSE IS NO longer my favourite house on the estate. I prefer the main house with all its grandeur and this is where I have chosen to live with Frank and Jack. The entire Royston art collection was found in the attic of Karl's gallery and every piece was re-hung in its original place. In the hallway I have a portrait of my mother and father and when I see them I am reminded that they are looking out for me, for me and my son Jack.

Jack does not remember anything about his time in the summer-house. The psychologist says it is perfectly normal for victims of trauma to blank out the details of their experiences.

Karl fell down the stairs at Hill Street that night and lingered on for weeks in a coma. Finally he slipped away. Jack thinks his dad died trying to save him. I can't disillusion him, not yet.

For the moment he believes Frank is his stepfather. We will tell him the truth, one day.

I was never charged with Nick's murder. A file was sent to the DPP, but it came back with the conclusion that I shot him in self-defence.

When I came back to live on the estate, I had the summer-house torn down.

'A scandalous waste,' I heard one of the gardeners say.